LESLIE E. HEATH

A DRAGON'S GIFT

A MOUNTAIN MAGIC FANTASY ADVENTURE

Credits:

Cover art: Natalie Narbonne at www.originalbookcoverdesigns.com

Editor: Elizabeth Prybylski

❋ Created with Vellum

This book is dedicated to my cat, Noodles, who refuses to ever allow my lap to get cold.

ACKNOWLEDGMENTS

I have to give a huge shout out to my editor, Elizabeth Prybylski for finding my errors and helping me set them right, especially when I seem to forget all comma rules and just stick them everywhere except where they're supposed to be. Sorry about that.

Also, I couldn't do this without my amazing team of beta readers, including Connie Powell, Marie DeJarnett, Cala Wrenn, Joyce Margosiak, and Tara Wallace, along with a few others who know who they are.

You all helped me find and fix a few major story problems, and the book is far better for your help.

NAP

*P*eridot shuffled along the trail, searching the sky above for signs of her favorite dragons. She stumbled and nearly fell when a low, menacing growl sounded near her feet. The noise brought her attention to the path, and all the strength left her legs. She sank to her knees beside a familiar animal lying on its side, bleeding from a deep wound near its shoulder.

"Sandulf! What happened?" She wrapped her arms around his chest and struggled to get the wolf on his feet, but he whimpered and lay back on the cold dirt. Dark blood soaked his gray fur and matted it close to his skin. It soaked her shirt and made his fur stick to her arms. She tugged again, but he didn't move, so she eased him back to the ground.

"All right, we'll have to do this here, then. Oh, I wish you could tell me what did this to you." She traced the odd oval wound with her finger, and the wolf licked at her hand. "I know it hurts. I'm going to try to make it better."

She pressed her hand to the wound the way she'd

learned in her first lesson in her grandmother's kitchen when she'd turned fourteen. That had been three years ago, but it felt like an eternity. She missed her grandmother's gentle manner of teaching. She'd been so much better than any of the teachers at the school. She turned her attention back to the wound beneath her palm before the memories could swamp her.

"You're lucky I've hurt myself so many times," She murmured to the injured wolf. "I've at least had a little practice with healing charms." She touched her right hand lightly to the wound and whispered, "confermo."

Nothing happened. The wolf whimpered again and lay his head on the ground. His legs trembled, and Peridot fought a wave of panic.

"No, don't give up. I'll get it right this time." She closed her eyes and pictured her grandmother. She had been shorter and smaller than Peridot with bright green eyes and yellowy-green hair that always made Peridot think of springtime. She pictured the old sprite in her kitchen, teaching Peridot how to do healing charms. She could almost hear the old woman's voice.

"Oh, of course." she touched her hand to the injury once more, concentrated on pulling the energy up from the ground, and said firmly, "confiervo." This time, a light the color of summer grass surrounded Peridot and the wolf, and the wound's edges turned pink and pulled together. The wolf whimpered and licked Peridot's hand with increasing vigor. When she finished, he sat up and licked her face.

Peridot laughed and swiped a hand across her cheek. Relief weakened her knees and she rested her cheek against his shoulder.

After a while, she whispered, "There. You'll be back to normal in no time. Let's get you home." She put her arms under his front legs and helped him to his feet, but he wobbled and stumbled. Peridot wrapped her arms around his neck and willed some of her strength into his body. She didn't know if it worked or if he'd just needed a moment to find his balance, but he took a step forward and then another. His pace was slow, his movements deliberate, but his tail wagged with each step.

As they made their way toward the wolves' den in the ruined city, Peridot puzzled over the odd wound. It had been a neat, clean oval, like something had punched a hole but much larger than a puncture from an eagle or a young dragon. She supposed it could have been from a full-grown dragon, but she doubted it. Those animals almost never bothered the wolves. They were too large to be prey to the eagles and too small to interest any but the weakest dragons. It hadn't been an arrow or knife injury, either, since those were usually long, narrow cuts in the skin with a lot of swelling underneath.

Absently, she ran her finger over the neat stitching on her quiver. Her mother had made it for her as a gift when she'd come of age, and it was by far the finest thing she owned. She counted the arrows and nodded. She had more than enough to defend herself and the wolves if it came to that. Maybe she'd find something suitable for supper along the way, too.

Peridot kicked a pebble along the trail behind the freshly-healed wolf and considered what to do next. "I should see you safely back to your pack and head home," she said aloud. The wolf ignored her and continued down the path, his head held high. "I'm supposed to be hunting. Mother's expecting visitors tomorrow."

This time, the wolf swung his great head around and gazed at her, his silver eyes boring into hers. His size struck her, and she fought a tiny shiver of fear. She sometimes forgot how large the wolves were. With him standing up, his head was at her eye level. His jaws could easily crush her skull if he chose to attack.

"Would you rather I stay with you for a while?" The wolf sighed and turned his attention back to the path. "I'll take that as a yes." She grinned at the wolf and followed him up the crumbling stairs that marked the entrance to the ruined city. Each step reached her knees, and she had to focus to keep her balance and make it safely to the top.

Sun-bleached stone columns stood tall like lonely sentinels protecting the entry against any foes, though whatever structure they had belonged to had long since decayed into sand. Such were the scenes throughout the city landscape. Large square areas stood empty and clear, only a few stones marking the corners of buildings or where the stairs had once been. In some places, tall spires held aloft sheets of an opaque material bleached white by the sun. Those interested Peridot the most. She couldn't imagine what they had once been or what the strange material was that didn't decay like the rest of the city.

"Father says there's whole mountains of that stuff on the plains," Peridot told the wolf. "He says it's a menace and that we should find a way to get rid of it."

The wolf ignored her but ambled faster toward the safety of home.

Peridot followed Sandulf down a crumbling alley and into the cave hidden behind the remains of another building. According to the records her father showed her, this had once been a building full of learning and knowledge. She wished she could see such a place, though she wasn't particularly good at learning from scrolls.

A low growl stopped her in her tracks and brought her attention to the path. She stopped in the opening to the cave, her shadow hiding a number of wolves sprawled on the cool stone floor. The growl wasn't coming from them but from a corner to her right. Peridot peered into the dim space and spotted several little wriggling animals behind another wolf who stood facing Peridot.

"Oh! You've had your babies! I won't bother them. Don't worry." She made her voice as soothing as she could and sidestepped away from the new mother.

The pack had accepted her three summers before, but she wasn't willing to push her luck with a new mother wolf. Her grandmother had always said there was no animal more dangerous than a mother protecting her babies, and Peridot had never seen anything to prove her wrong.

As Peridot moved away from the newborn pups, the mother settled down, lying in front of the babies. She kept her eyes on Peridot but lay her head on the ground. Peridot wished she had brought bits of sausage or meat from last night's supper, but she hadn't planned to visit the wolves that day.

That thought reminded Peridot why she had come, and she squinted into the cave's darker corners, searching for the injured wolf. The charm had healed the skin and muscle, but the wound would ache for a few days. She found him curled up beside his mate, a pretty female with warm brown eyes and gray and brown markings on her back that looked like the drawings of striped horses in the giants' books. Peridot moved through the cave, patting and stroking each wolf she passed and murmuring words of encouragement and love to each one.

"There now," she said when she reached Sandulf. "Getting home makes everything better, doesn't it?"

The wolf laid his head on his mate and chuffed softly.

Peridot laid a hand on his head and rubbed behind his ears. "All right, well, since you're home with your family now, I'd better get back to hunting. I'll be in trouble I don't have a deer or ram by sundown."

Sandulf whimpered and raised his head, meeting Peridot's gaze. His eyes held a sadness and fear that melted her resolve.

Peridot laughed and played with his warm, soft ears. "All right. I'll stay for a little while. You need a little reassurance, don't you?" She sat down beside Sandulf, her back against the warm fur of another wolf. She ran her fingers through the long, thick fur where the wound had been, rubbing gentle circles over the area.

The wolf groaned and dropped his head onto his mate's back. Peridot chuckled and rubbed that spot again. "You like that? All right. How about if I recite my lessons while I massage your shoulder?" The wolf didn't move but heaved a great sigh and relaxed completely under her touch.

"If you say so. All right. Now, mother says I should practice my charms more, but I can't do that in here with the new babies, so let's go over maths instead."

She spent the next hour writing maths problems in the dirt with her fingers and solving them with the solutions her mother had taught her. She'd never liked maths, though, so she soon grew bored and doodled in the sand, instead.

Peridot shifted, but Sandulf snored softly, letting her know he'd fallen asleep. Unwilling to wake him, she laid her head on his side and listened to the *thumpa, thumpa* of his heart and the gentle whoosh of air going in and out of his lungs. The warmth and softness of his fur lulled her into relaxing further.

"I really should get going," she murmured, pulling the bow and quiver off her back and leaning them against the wall. "Mother will be angry if I stay much longer." Instead of getting up, Peridot heaved a great yawn and fell asleep snuggled between the giant wolves beneath the ruined city.

The great wolf stretched and moved. Peridot's head hit the floor, and the pain jerked her out of her dreams. She rubbed her head and sat up, blinking at the wolves stirring in the dim space around her.

"Oh, no." The cave was almost completely dark, which meant the sun had either set or was about to. Her mother would be furious. "I'll be back soon."

Peridot grabbed her bow and quiver and slung them onto her back as she ran out of the cave. She leapt down the crumbling stairs and onto the packed dirt and gravel trail that wound through the forest and sprinted toward the village. She'd only made it a hundred paces when her bare toe caught a root. She flew forward, falling face-first onto the hard earth. Her hands, knees, and elbows burned and ached, but Peridot jumped up and continued her mad dash toward home, spitting sand and dirt as she ran. Between steps, she tried to come up with a suitable excuse for having nothing to show for her day in the forest. She stopped at the first trap she'd set that morning, hoping for at least a rabbit or fox, but it stood empty and untouched.

Well, not exactly untouched, she thought, looking closer at the trap.

Something had taken the bait, and blood spattered the ground near the trap. No signs of a struggle marred the ground; the leaves and sticks looked untouched. No footprints or tracks led away from the trap.

Puzzled, Peridot left the trap and continued her rush toward home. She had four more traps to check, each set for mid-sized game such as the raccoons and opossums that reached her knees or foxes that stood to her hip. One such animal would be enough to feed her family and whatever guests her mother expected, but the next trap had also been emptied of its quarry. Again, there were no signs of anything leaving the area.

She cursed under her breath and kicked the empty steel trap. It snapped shut with a clang, and its shiny teeth narrowly missed her foot. Cowed, she shot it a look and left it as it lay. She didn't have time to reset it, and she had nothing to use as bait.

The next two traps were the same. Frustration and panic curled long fingers through Peridot's stomach and squeezed. She glanced at the orange-streaked sky. It wasn't quite dark yet. She still had time to hunt. If she moved quickly, she could get something to satisfy her mother and still make it home before darkness obscured the path and ushered in the hunting hours of the deadliest predators.

She crouched beside the trap and pressed a hand to her chest. Her heart beat out a frantic rhythm against it. She'd never get close enough to an animal to make a kill while she was so upset; the animals would sense her panic and flee. She closed her eyes, pictured her favorite spot in the ruined city, and focused on her breathing. Somewhere nearby, an owl hooted. A gentle breeze rustled the leaves. The pungent scent of dung wafted over her.

Peridot opened her eyes and drew her bow off her back. Nocking an arrow, she crept off in the direction of the odor. It had to be fresh to smell so strong. She sniffed the air, trying to decipher what sort of animal had been there. A carnivore of some sort. Maybe a fox.

Excitement rose in her chest, but Peridot fought off the feeling. She had to stay calm. She moved through the forest with the grace of a cougar--silent, swift, and deadly.

The trees thinned, and Peridot slowed. Ahead, the burble of water announced she'd reached the stream. Animals gathered there to drink and catch the fish in the shallows—and larger carnivores came to hunt the smaller animals. She paused behind a thick sycamore tree and listened for sounds of movement in the clearing. Squirrels chittered and jumped above her, but she couldn't hear anything beyond the tree except the running water.

She drew a deep breath and let it out. Ever so slowly, she leaned her head past the bark, peering into the darkening space. Thirty paces in front of her, a huge brown bear leaned over the flowing water, poised to swipe at the fish swimming through. Peridot gasped. The soft sound alerted the bear to her presence, and it swung a long-snouted head around.

The bear spun with alarming speed and moved toward Peridot's hiding place. Its slow, unconcerned movements lulled her into a false sense of ease until it crossed the clearing at a blistering speed. It drew too close, and she fired the arrow she'd nocked. It connected with the bear's right shoulder. Unfortunately, the pain only angered the animal. Its roar vanished into the deepening darkness, absorbed by the forest and the evening mist.

Peridot turned to run, and all her mother's lessons blurred in her mind. What had she said to do to get away from a bear? Climb? No, bears could climb trees. She knew running wasn't the best plan, since bears were so much faster than sprites. The animal crashed through the forest behind her, gaining on her with every step she took. Desperate, she spun, raised her empty right hand toward the towering animal, and shouted, "procrusus!"

A blinding stream of violet light erupted from her hand and surrounded the bear.

"No! Precursos!"

Nothing happened that time except a soft rumble in the distance. Luckily, the violet light distracted the bear, and Peridot slipped away into the forest as quickly and silently as she could. She hoped that once the light charm wore off the beast wouldn't be able to track her by her scent.

Without warning, the cover of the trees gave way to a wide, open shelf. The distant rumble grew to a roar, and the ground crumbled away. Peridot cursed her own misuse of charms and skidded to a stop, but not soon enough. She tumbled off the edge and dropped the eight feet to the hard ground below. She tucked herself into a ball but landed hard. She couldn't hold in the grunt that escaped on impact. Something hard jabbed into her side, and a cool draft alerted her to a new tear in her pants.

The impact knocked the wind out of her, and she lay

perfectly still and waited until she could breathe normally again. The night wind ruffled her hair and drifted into places that should have been covered by her favorite outfit. Somewhere above her, the bear roared, its fury fading into the night.

An uneasy silence fell over the forest, and Peridot held her breath and waited until the small creatures chirped and chattered before she stood and brushed the dirt and gravel from her hands. A small cut burned on her right arm, and the night air stung a scrape along her left knee. She sighed. She'd ruined her favorite pair of linen summer pants, but she was overall unharmed. She could heal her wounds on the way home. Unfortunately, her bow hadn't fared as well. She'd landed atop the thin wood, and it had snapped in half. She held the splintered ends in her hands and considered possible ways to repair it, but it was useless. Tears flooded her eyes and blurred her vision at the damage to her favorite bow, but she blinked them back. She still had to get home, and the last hint of daylight had faded into night, and with it had come a heavy mist.

The mist hid everything but the ground beneath her feet, but Peridot knew the way home. Forcing the thoughts of cougars and other night hunters from her mind, she ran her hands though the tall grasses and charged through the valley though she stopped once to concentrate on healing the small cuts and scrapes. Twenty minutes later, she followed the left fork through the village gates and onto the dusty road where she'd grown up. Her mother, Lorenza, stood outside their home, watching and waiting.

When she caught sight of her daughter, Lorenza raised

the lamp higher. "Peridot! There you are! What took you so long? We thought you'd be back hours ago." She cut off when Peridot drew near. "What happened to you? And your bow? Where's our dinner for tomorrow's guests?"

Peridot ducked her head and dropped her arms to her sides. "I... I tried, Mother. I really did. Someone's been robbing my traps again. Every one of them had signs of a catch, but they were all empty. Even the bait was gone."

"How many times have we told you not to use those traps for catching food? They just make the meat taste gamey and off. It's a lazy habit you've developed, and it's time you started hunting properly again." Her mother's gaze took in Peridot's disheveled appearance, and she added, "And you've ruined your best outfit." Her mother clucked her tongue and ushered Peridot into the small stone-walled house.

A fire blazed on the hearth and warmed the tiny space. Peridot sighed and relaxed a degree. Warmth burned in her stiff fingers and stung her cheeks. She hadn't realized how cold she'd gotten. She walked slowly, keeping her head down, her eyes on the brown braided rug that covered the stone and dirt floor, hoping her mother wouldn't notice her missing cloak. She silently vowed to search the forest for it tomorrow.

Peridot raised her head and glanced around the cozy room. Their home was a fraction of the size the buildings in the ruined city must have been, but it was large enough for her to live comfortably with her parents, her sister, and her brother. Worn tapestries and blankets hung on the walls and covered the windows to help keep the warmth in and ward off the night's chill.

A bulbous, black pot bubbled on the potbellied stove

in the corner. Three oil lamps suspended over the small round table cast a warm yellow light over the room. Chairs and rugs lined the interior of the central room, and four smaller rooms extended from the main living space. Those were the family's bedrooms and the one small dressing room they shared.

Peridot headed for the dressing room. After her encounter with the bear, she needed to answer nature's call. Narrow shelves lined the wall beside the dressing room, each stacked with piles of charcoal lumps that had once been excrement. That was the first charm any sprite learned to do—turning their waste products into clean charcoal that could be used to cook their food and heat their homes.

"Peri, you ever coming out?" Her brother, Kent, called through the heavy curtain. "We're all starving to death in here. You're holding up dinner."

"Just a minute. Let me wash the dirt off my hands," Peridot grumbled. She grimaced and poured cold water from the pitcher over her palms. Moving quickly, she rubbed to remove the worst of the grime and blood and dried her hands on a small towel. She held her hands up to her face, checking for any injuries that still needed attention. The scrapes had healed to thin pink lines beneath the tell-tale stains. A few faint bruises showed on her palms and fingers, but no swelling marred her fingers, and her knuckles all bent as they should.

When she emerged from the dressing room, she ducked her head under her family's angry stares.

"Peridot," her mother's tone was at once endlessly patient and furious. "What are we supposed to serve our guests tomorrow night if we have no meat for the pot?"

She pressed her lips into a thin line and waited for an answer with her hands braced on her narrow hips.

Peridot raised a hand and opened her mouth to speak, but her mother cut her off.

"And don't give me that excuse about the traps again. You were gone all day. You had more than enough time to hunt."

"But it's true! Someone *is* robbing the traps. I caught something in at least three of them, but they're all empty."

Peridot's mother turned her back to her and stirred the stewpot with a long-handled ladle. "We'll ignore the fact that you're not supposed to be using those traps for now. But what did you do with the rest of the day *after* you'd set the traps? You clearly weren't watching them."

"Well... I... That big gray wolf got hurt somehow. I healed the gash in his shoulder and stayed with him until he was more comfortable, that's all."

Her father's voice held none of his wife's patience. "Peridot, how many times have we told you to leave those dogs alone? They're dangerous!" He stood and crossed the room to stand beside Peridot's mother. "One of these days they'll get hungry and decide you look like a tasty meal."

"No, they won't! They're friendly!" Peridot frowned at her tone and worked to modulate her voice. "They love me as much as I love them. You even told me about the pictures they found in the city of the wolves with the giants. You said they had pictures everywhere of the wolves sitting with their favorite giant—"

"That has nothing to do with it. Nothing at all," her father roared. "You're not a giant. There are no more giants, which is why their cities are all crumbling, and their dogs roam the countryside. You're a sprite, less than half the size of a giant. Those dogs will have you for dinner, and then where will that leave your family?" He set his hand on his wife's shoulder but didn't take his eyes off Peridot. "You kids insist on calling them wolves, but they're not, not truly. The real wolves don't have markings like the giants' dogs. They're pure gray, and they're more predictable, too. Those dogs could turn on you in a heartbeat."

Again, Peridot opened her mouth to respond only to be cut off by her angry mother. "Forget the dogs or wolves or whatever you want to call them, Peridot. They're not yours to tend. What are we going to do without meat for tomorrow?"

Heat flushed Peridot's face, making her ears burn. "I'm sorry, Mother. I really am. I'll go back out at dawn and get us a fox."

"Very well. Let's eat before the stew burns." Her mother sounded more tired than angry, and Peridot sighed. Her mother hated conflict at the dinner table, so she'd drop the matter until later.

Angene screwed up her face and flipped her long pink hair over her shoulder. "Great job, Peridot. It's not like anyone was counting on you or anything," she sneered, keeping her voice low so their mother wouldn't hear. "I would hope my own sister would make sure I have something decent to serve a new suitor."

Peridot didn't answer. Instead, she focused on keeping her hands steady. She dipped the iron ladle into the pot, careful to avoid the edges, and filled her bowl. Without looking away from the steaming stew, she carried her dinner to the table and scooped a spoonful into her mouth without waiting for it to cool.

Burning pain brought tears to her eyes, but at least it hid her embarrassment and shame. She hadn't planned to find an injured wolf, and she hadn't meant to fall asleep with him. And her encounter with the bear certainly hadn't been on her agenda for the day.

She ate her supper as quickly as she could and retreated to her bedroom as soon as she'd emptied and washed her bowl.

Alone in the small bedroom she shared with Angene, Peridot pulled out the straw-colored fine linen gown she'd been working on for Bryoni's birthday party. She'd pulled off all the old, childish lace and was replacing it with a broad green ribbon she'd bought for the occasion. She stabbed the needle in and out of the fabric, taking her frustrations out on the delicate garment.

She'd spent months helping Bryoni plan this party, and now it was only a fortnight away. Her gown was almost finished, but she still had hours' worth of work to do on the embroidered dragon tapestry she was making for her best friend's birthday gift.

While she worked, she imagined the village square all decked out in lamps and vines. A table full of cakes and sweets would sit at the back, along with pitchers of lemonade made from lemons grown in Bryoni's father's greenhouse, and large containers of cool water from the spring. Bryoni's brothers and their friends would play the music while their guests twirled in circles around the open dance floor like the pictures they'd seen of the giants' parties. At the mental image, some of Peridot's discomfort over the hunting debacle ebbed, replaced by a thrill of excitement.

KENT

*P*eridot lost herself in the work of sewing and daydreaming about the party. It took several moments for her to come out of the fog when her mother's voice drifted through the curtain in the doorway.

"Kent, would it be too much trouble to run out and get a couple of raccoons? They've been scavenging in the gardens every night for weeks. You shouldn't have to go far. Besides, getting rid of them will mean more vegetables for us this summer."

"Yes, Mother." Kent's voice wasn't as quiet as their mother's. "But Peri said she'd go at dawn. Shouldn't we let her fix her own mess?"

Something metal clattered against the counter, and Peridot flinched at the unexpected noise. "She'll just end up wandering off to check on those dogs again. No, we need to make sure we have something to serve. This could be Angene's best chance to catch a husband."

"Yes, Mother," Kent repeated.

Before Kent could gather his bow and arrow and don

his boots, Peridot launched herself through the doorway, barely pausing to shove the curtain aside.

"I'll go," she announced. "It's my fault someone has to go out in that wind and rain, it might as well be me that fixes it."

Kent shook his head, but Peridot ignored him and turned to her mother. "Really, Mother, I'll go."

Her mother shared a meaningful look with her father, then turned back to Peridot. "No. You'll stay here and clean yourself up. Lord Maksym's on his way over. You make yourself presentable for him––and no whining," she added when Peridot started to protest. "I swear, I don't know what you have against that man. He's been nothing but good to us." She dried the ladle she'd been washing and hung it on its hook beside the fireplace.

Peridot bit the inside of her cheek until she tasted blood, turned on her heel, and stomped back to her room.

"Oh, Peridot," Angene's taunting voice carried from the main room. "You'd have better prospects for husbands if you'd behave as a proper young lady should. When was the last time you attended your lessons?"

Fuming, Peridot threw off her torn, mud-stained clothes and replaced them with the high-necked, loose-fitting dress she usually wore when Lord Maksym, her father's boss and the local lord, came to visit. It was a horrid pea-soup green with a mustard sash that made Peridot want to vomit. It looked even worse on her. It hung loose as a flour sack and leant her skin a sickly-looking, sallow tone.

When she'd dressed, she dragged her brush through her tangled lilac hair. She pulled out bits of leaves and grass. Dirt and sand dusted her shoulders, and she brushed it away without a care for any streaks or marks it might have left. She didn't bother braiding ribbons into her hair, as her mother would have preferred, but instead pulled the length of it into a severe bun at the base of her skull. She stood back and surveyed her appearance in the looking glass that leaned against the wall by her bed. She looked like a forty-year-old spinster rather than the seventeen-year-old she was. Satisfied, she gave a little smile and swept out the door into the main room.

Her father frowned when he saw her. "Really, Dot," he said, his voice pained. "Couldn't you try to look like you're happy to see him? He's made it quite clear he's interested in courting you, and you couldn't ask for a better match."

Outrage freed Peridot's tongue and brought a new flush to her cheeks. "A better match? Anyone would be a better match." She shook her head and flounced to her favorite spot. She sat on the new brown rug and drew her knees to her chest. "He's twice your age, which makes him old enough to be my grandfather. And I heard he beat his last wife to death. Why would you wish that on me?"

"That's quite enough." Her mother's face flushed scarlet. "I'll not have you spreading rumors like that."

Peridot fought the tears welling in her eyes and hated the fact that she cried when she was frustrated or angry. "But it's true!" She swiped at her face. The rebellious tears only served to make her angrier.

"No, it is not. That is the end of this discussion. I'm going to see where your brother's got off to." Her father stood and stalked out the door, slamming it behind him and rattling the windows.

"You know it's true," Peridot cried to her mother.

"Otherwise, why wouldn't he allow any healers near her? He wanted to keep his abuse hidden, that's why!" She added.

"She died in childbirth," her mother whispered, "And he was so broken up about it that he didn't call the doctor for three days. He spent that time at her bedside, calling her name and crying according to the servants. Now, you'll keep a civil tongue while he's here, and I won't listen to this nonsense from you anymore."

Peridot dropped her eyes to the floor to hide the desperation welling in her gut. She couldn't bear to continue the argument. Instead, she retrieved the embroidered dragon tapestry she'd been working on from her bedroom and sat at the table where she worked silently until a knock sounded at the door.

The room went cold, but Peridot couldn't tell if that was because the open door let in the cold wind or if the blood had drained from her face and hands. Lord Maksym stood in the doorway, chortling and addressing each of the room's occupants. His faded blue hair bounced on top of his head, too long to lie flat like a proper gentleman's hair but too short to wave gracefully like the men she admired.

"Peridot, there you are, my dear." He strode across the room and dropped into the chair beside her. "I came by just to see you and assure you that you have nothing to worry about tomorrow night. The young lady who will be accompanying me is my niece, Ridley. She's been begging to come out and see the mountains, so I've agreed to introduce her around."

Peridot ground her teeth at his overly affectionate manner. Why did she hate this man so much? She couldn't exactly explain it, but he made the little hairs on the back of her neck stand on end, and she always did everything she could to avoid being alone with him.

"Oh, I've made a fresh cake with carrots from our garden. Would you like some?" Peridot's mother produced a lightly browned cake from beneath the counter and placed it on the table with a flourish.

The door swung open, admitting another blast of frigid air along with Peridot's father. "That looks lovely, Lorenza. I'd love some. Maybe something hot to drink, too, perhaps?"

"Oh, yes," Lord Maksym cooed. "Something hot would be perfect. My hands are quite frozen from that wind. Or maybe... Perhaps Lady Peridot would like to warm them for me?"

Peridot pretended not to hear him, focusing instead on a particularly tricky section of her embroidery. She stabbed the needle through the fabric in a rhythmic motion, tuning out everything around her. Or so she thought.

"I have just the thing," Peridot's mother chimed in, bustling across the room. "I made some cider from the last of our apples. It'll be warm in a moment." She pulled a ceramic pot out of the cupboard, poured the opaque amber liquid into the kettle, and set it on the potbelly stove.

A chair scraped across the floor. Something warm puffed across Peridot's ear, and the smell of onions assaulted her nose. "You don't have to pretend to be so shy, my dear. I suspect by the beginning of summer we'll be able to announce our engagement."

Peridot's stomach rolled, and she fought the urge to

gag and run. Instead, she kept her eyes studiously fixed on the tapestry in her lap and refused to let Lord Maksym goad her into overreacting. The silence filled the room, a palpable, uncomfortable blanket weighing down everyone within its reach.

"Peridot," Angene's voice sounded entirely too cheerful. "Why don't you tell Lord Maksym that amusing story from your lessons last month? I'm sure he'd find it as funny as we all did."

Peridot stabbed the needle into her embroidery. "I'd rather not. It wasn't funny then, and it wouldn't be funny now."

"Here we are," her mother interjected. "This cider's hot, so be careful." She set five mismatched teacups on the table and filled each to the brim with steaming cider. As soon as she'd finished, she served each person a slice of carrot cake and took her seat across from Peridot.

With the others filling the space at the table, Lord Maksym scooted away from Peridot. He usually reserved comments about courting for her ears only.

Relief stole the strength from her arms and left her weak and tired. Peridot turned her attention to the dessert. Her mother had long been the best cook in the village, and the cake certainly didn't disappoint. It was soft and moist, richly spiced, but not overly sweet, and the cinnamon glaze added the perfect finish. She ate it all, then took a swig of her cider, which had cooled while she enjoyed the cake.

"Angene," Lord Maksym crooned, "Did I tell you we got a new set of books for the library? They're a dozen books from the giants' city, translated to modern language so they're easier to read."

Angene looked up, her pale blue hair swinging over her shoulder. "Oh? Which ones? I thought I'd read all the books from the city."

Unable to resist, Peridot raised her eyes to Lord Maksym's face. When he met her gaze, she shifted her eyes away to her room where she had four books hidden under her mattress.

"It's a series of novels that detail what life and love was like for the giants at the height of their reign." Lord Maksym turned his attention back to Angene. "It truly is a shame they extincted themselves. I think they would have been fascinating neighbors."

"I don't know about that. Our ancestors had to keep themselves hidden, didn't they?" Peridot tried to contain the retort, but she just couldn't help herself.

"Did they?" Peridot's father's voice held a note of warning. "The giants wrote several books about our kind, about sprites and elves and dwarves and dragons and all the other races that thought they'd stayed out of sight."

If she'd been among friends, Peridot could have debated this point for hours. As it was, however, she wanted to see Lord Maksym's visit end as quickly as possible.

"Of course, how could I have forgotten?" She took another gulp of cider and turned her attention back to her embroidery.

"You know, I have a whole collection of those books in my personal library, Peridot. You're welcome to borrow them any time you like." Lord Maksym smiled graciously, and Angene simpered.

"Oh, that sounds lovely." Angene smiled.

Peridot fought the urge to roll her eyes.

"This cake is amazing, Lorenza," Peridot's father said. "Did you do something different with it this time?"

"Oh, yes, I added a bit of applesauce and more cinnamon than usual. Can you really tell the difference?" Peridot's mother beamed. She stood and began clearing the dishes. "Can I interest you in another cup of cider, Lord Maksym?"

"No, thank you, Lorenza. I really should get home. My carriage should be arriving any moment with my niece, and I expect my nephew before midnight. I do appreciate your hospitality."

He stood and strolled to the door. "I'm sure you're looking forward to tomorrow evening quite as much as I am. I shall see you then."

With an absurdly formal bow, he pulled open the door and swept out into the night.

As soon as the door closed, Peridot sighed and flopped her embroidery onto the table.

"Really, Peridot. I don't understand you. You couldn't ask for a better suitor." Her mother stacked the dishes in the basin to wash in the morning.

"I don't know, Mother." Peridot sighed, exhaustion rolling over her in a wave. "Maybe it's just that he's so old. I'd really prefer to marry someone closer to my own age."

"If you want a suitor your age, why won't you go to your lessons?" Angene's sneer made it clear she wasn't trying to be helpful.

Peridot pressed her lips into a line and refused to take the bait. The men in the village didn't attend the same lessons as the women, anyway, but pointing that out would only spark more discussion, and Peridot didn't have the energy to argue.

"He's a good man, Dot," her father said gently, using the nickname he'd given her as a small child. "I spend enough time with him to know. He takes care of his home and his people."

"You work for him. That's nowhere near the same as marrying him! I need to change clothes. This dress is itchy." She stalked off toward her bedroom.

"I don't know why you always wear that hideous thing when he comes to visit, anyway," her mother said just before she stepped through the curtain. "Didn't I make you new dresses this winter? Why won't you wear one of those?"

Peridot poked her head through the door to answer. "You did, Mother. And I do wear them, just not for him."

"Difficult. She's just being difficult." Her father's voice carried through the curtain. "She'll come around. Just give her time. Maybe we should have him over more often, so she can see how good a man he really is."

"That's not a bad idea, but maybe we shouldn't push too hard. She's awfully stubborn, and I don't want to jeopardize your job if she makes a fool of herself."

"I promise I won't make a fool of myself if I can get a rich suitor, Mother."

Peridot rolled her eyes and grumbled, "As if she needs to try."

Instead of putting on her dressing gown, she pulled on a heavy sweater and thick breeches, slid her feet into her warmest shoes, and swung her old, worn cloak over her shoulders. She needed some room to think, and she wanted to check on Kent. The image of the wolf's odd wound and the angry bear flashed through her mind. She hoped nothing had happened to him. It shouldn't have taken him so long to catch a raccoon by the garden.

Peridot grabbed her old bow and quiver off the hooks

on the wall and hurried past her family without a word. She swept out into the night and gathered her cloak close, lest it be caught when she let the door swing shut behind her. The cold took her breath away, especially after the stuffy heat of the house, but the bitter wind she'd fought on the way home had died down to a gentle breeze. She stood still beside the house and waited for her eyes to adjust to the dark.

The half-moon overhead provided enough light to see the dirt road and all the neighboring homes. Peridot stalked around the house toward the garden, searching the ground for any sign of the raccoon or her brother, but only the bushes moved in the rhythm of the breeze. She gave a silent thanks to the mountain for calming the biting wind she'd fought earlier in the night.

"Peridot!" Her mother's voice brought her up short, and Peridot changed course. "What are you doing out here so late?"

"I wanted a bit of target practice," she quipped. "It looks like I'm going hunting at dawn, and I haven't shot this bow in ages."

Her mother's delicate features puckered into a frown. "Where's your brother gone off to? He was supposed to be catching the raccoons from the garden, not running off to hunt."

"I don't know where he is since you wouldn't let me go with him, and Father didn't say a word after he went to look for him." Peridot winced. She needed to be more mindful of how she spoke to her mother, but she couldn't help herself. "You wanted me to stay and make nice with Father's nasty old boss so you can live in the big, fancy house. I won't marry him, Mother. I won't."

"That's enough. We're talking about your brother. Where is he?"

Peridot stepped to the right, lining herself up with the target, and nocked an arrow. "I told you, I don't know where he is. You wouldn't let me go with him, remember?"

Thwack. She let the arrow fly. It hit on the line between the bullseye and the ring surrounding it.

"Damn. My aim's off." Peridot brushed her hair out of her eyes, tucked the troublesome strand behind her ear, and pulled out another arrow.

"Watch your language. You know better than to talk like that."

"You don't have to watch." Peridot took aim again. "I save my 'proper lady' behavior for your miserable guests. Here, it's just me and the target, and I say whatever comes to mind."

Thwack. This time, the arrow hit dead center. "Better. I wonder why this one pulls to the left. Maybe I've gotten a bit taller since I last used it."

Thwack. Thwack. Thwack.

She fired several arrows in quick succession, practicing as if she were chasing an animal with arrows. A perfect row of fletchings grew out of the target.

"Would you stop that and listen to me?" Her mother's stern voice brooked no argument, so Peridot lowered her bow.

She stood still, waiting. A strong gust of wind whistled between the houses and whipped at her cloak, but Peridot ignored it.

When her mother said nothing more, Peridot shifted her weight forward. "Do you want me to go looking for him? I have no idea which way he's gone. It might be better to wait until morning when I can find his tracks."

"No. I'd rather you come inside and get cleaned up. I want you looking your best for our guests tomorrow night. Lord Maksym talked to your father today. We've given our permission for him to court you formally."

"Why? Why would you do that?" Peridot lifted the bow and nocked another arrow.

"You'll receive his courtship gracefully or else." Her mother grabbed the bow just as Peridot released the arrow. It flew wild, missing the target and planting among the bushes in the garden.

Fury filled Peridot's eyes, and she met her mother's gaze without fear. "No, I will not. I won't pretend to like him, Mother."

"If that's the way you want to be, then that's fine." Her mother nodded once and crossed her arms over her chest. "You won't be going to Bryoni's party, or any other party that comes up, until you can be reasonable."

The words hit Peridot like a blow to the gut. "Mother! How could you? I've been helping her plan that party for months. I always help her."

"Look, I know there are better looking men around, but that's not the point. None of them have shown much interest in you. So, you can either make the match that will best benefit your family, or you can give up your other social engagements. That's final."

Her mother spun and walked away, and Peridot turned back to the target. She put all her fury into the bow, shooting every arrow in her quiver before wiping the tears from her face and moving to retrieve her arrows. She gathered the ones from the target and went to search for the one she'd lost in the garden before planting herself and shooting all her arrows again. Her shoulders burned and her upper back ached from the effort.

She repeated the process until she hit the center with every shot. Sweat dripped down her back by the time she'd finished.

FRIENDS

The moon had marched across the sky, and the wind chilled the sweat slicking Peridot's skin and dampening her clothes. She plucked her arrows out of the target and dropped them into her quiver. Not quite ready to face her family, she set off for Bryoni's house one street over.

She tapped two knuckles on the yellow wooden door and waited. The door opened a crack.

She couldn't fight a smile when Bryoni's pink hair and soft brown eyes peeked out through the tiny opening. "Bryoni! Can I come in?"

"Of course." Bryoni frowned but opened the door.

The house was almost double the size of Peridot's and had stone tiles covering the floors. Peridot hesitated just inside the door. Bryoni's parents and brother sat in plush chairs in the main room, all staring at Peridot with curious expressions.

"Dot! Is everything all right dear? You look upset."

Bryoni's mother asked. Her hair had gone pure white as she'd aged which emphasized her delicate, pointy features and brown eyes which looked exactly like Bryoni's.

"I'm all right. I just wanted to talk to Bry. Is that all right? I hope I'm not interrupting anything."

"Oh, that's fine dear. You'll find the sitting room in the back empty, but you'll probably want to start a fire. It certainly has turned cold tonight."

"Yes, ma'am, it has." Peridot shivered and followed Bryoni through the house and into the dark, cold sitting room which stayed closed off from the rest of the house.

"I wish my mother was as nice as yours," Peridot said as Bryoni lit the lamps. "Your mother always seems happy to see you and never says anything unkind about anyone."

"Oh, nonsense." Bryoni laughed. She held a hand out in front of her and murmured, "Ignis embre," and a tiny flame caught a corner of the front log. Moments later, a blazing fire roared to life on the hearth.

Peridot watched in amazement. "Could you teach me to do that?"

Bryoni laughed again. "You'd know how to do that if you'd come to lessons every now and then." At Peridot's hurt expression, she added, "But I'd be happy to teach you this week. So, what happened? What made you come over here so late?"

"My father's given Lord Maksym permission to court me openly." Peridot buried her face in her hands and fought back a new wave of tears.

"Oh, no." Bryoni's horrified tone matched Peridot's feelings on the subject.

"And that's not the half of it," Peridot said between her fingers. "When I told my mother that I won't marry him, she said I can't go to your party or any other party until I can 'be more reasonable!' What am I going to do?" She dropped her hands and met Bryoni's shocked gaze.

"But the party's next week! I still need your help with the flowers and all the food and flowers and, and…everything!"

"I know! She's just being awful. She says I have to make the match that best benefits my family, but I don't care about that. They certainly aren't willing to do anything for me. Besides, I don't care if I'm poor my whole life as long as I don't have to marry Lord Maksym!"

Hot tears flooded down Peridot's face, and she fell silent. Bryoni nudged her over to the bearskin chaise and sat next to her, putting an arm around her shoulders.

"And that's not even all of it," Peridot wailed after a long pause. "Someone's been robbing my traps again, so I came home without anything for tomorrow's supper, and Mother sent Kent out in the dark to catch something to serve Lord Maksym and his friends, but he never came back. I checked for him in the garden, but he wasn't there! I don't know where he's gone off to, but something weird's going on in the forest. I hope he didn't run into the bear I tangled with earlier."

"It sounds like you've had quite a day. Who do you think is robbing your traps? Wasn't it the twins down the street, Owen and Wilson, the last time?"

"I don't think it's them this time, but it might be. This time, whoever did it reset the traps with no bait. When Owen did it, he just left it closed."

"So, who do you think it is?"

"I don't know. But there's more." She told Bryoni all about the wolf's unusual injury and how she'd healed him and stayed to see him comfortable. Then she explained how she'd fallen asleep and run into the bear on the way home.

"Oh, you *have* had an interesting day. Hold on, let me get the kettle. Some sassafras tea'll help settle your nerves." Bryoni stood and moved toward the door.

"That sounds perfect. Do you have any honey?" Peridot scooted closer to the fire and warmed her cold fingers.

Bry nodded. "I think so. I'll ask Mother."

Alone in the plush sitting room, Peridot swiped her hands over her wet cheeks. Bryoni hadn't said much, but she felt better just for telling someone else her troubles. She sniffled softly and watched the flames dancing in the fireplace. A growing knot of worry tensed her stomach. Where had Kent gone? It wasn't like him to wander off in the dark. He wasn't as comfortable with the animals outside the village as Peridot was, so he preferred staying close to the houses.

Minutes later, Bryoni returned with a tea tray. The sweet scent of the sassafras helped calm Peridot even before she'd tasted her cup.

"Oh, Mother found a bit of honey, too. None of us like it much, so you can have as much as you want."

"Thank you." Peridot spooned a huge dollop of honey into her teacup and stirred. She raised the cup to her lips and sighed at the calming taste of the sweet tea.

"What am I going to do?" she asked Bryoni when she'd finished half her cup. "I can't stand the thought of encouraging Lord Maksym, but I have to go to your party."

"I don't know. What if you pretend to like him for a

few days, just to get through the party, then let him know you're not interested?"

Peridot sighed. "I considered that, but it just feels so, I don't know, dishonest. And gross."

The two sat in silence for a long while, and Peridot stared into the fire as if all the answers were there for her to decipher.

"You know, that family from the coast started lessons yesterday." A thoughtful crease appeared between Bryoni's eyebrows. "The men came, too, and a couple of them are close to our age. Maybe you should start coming so you can get to know some of them. Your mother might back off a bit if you had some other prospects." Bryoni gave a sly smile. "I've asked one of them, Henry, to be my date for my party."

Peridot couldn't hide her surprise. "That's amazing! Did he accept? What's he like?" She paused and asked, "They're going to lessons already? Have they shown any powers yet? I've never heard of anyone starting so soon. They just moved in a few months ago."

"Not yet, but they're really nice, and they're eager to learn. I think they're hoping they get powers soon, so they can fit in a bit better. Wouldn't it be lovely if you could learn with them? Henry already said yes to me, and he has a brother one year older than he is, and another a year younger."

"Ha, ha. I know more than you're implying." Peridot ignored the comment about the boys. "I'm getting really good at healing charms." Peridot poured the last of the tea into her cup and downed it in one swallow. "I healed Sandulf in two tries today. And he could walk again and everything." She grinned and set her teacup on the narrow table.

Bryoni smiled back. "I'm no good at healing, but I keep trying. I guess we all have our own talents, don't we? Still, you'd benefit from coming to lessons more. You're spending too much time on the mountain, and people are starting to talk."

"Oh? Like what? Is that why Mother's acting so weird about Lord Maksym?"

"I've heard whispers, though of course no one says anything to me, since everyone knows we're friends." Bryoni paused and frowned. "They're saying you prefer wild animals to people and that you're turning wild--like that man who went into the forest and lived there for decades without ever coming back to town."

Peridot cocked her head and examined her friend. "What man? I don't know who you're talking about."

"See? You should come to lessons, so you can learn about our history."

Peridot shook her head. "I know about our history. I've read all the books in the library."

Bryoni rolled her eyes. "Most of those are the giants' fairy tales. I still can't believe so many people believe they're true."

"I know, but there's a lot of our history hidden in those stories. According to our ancestors, the giants didn't know we existed then, but if they didn't know, then how did they include our kind in so many of their stories?"

"There's more of our history out in the open in our lessons. Really, Dot, how do you expect to fit in with soci-ety--regardless of who you marry--if you don't even know the stories?"

Peridot groaned. "All right, I get it. I'll start coming to lessons more often. Not every day, though. How about twice a week?"

"You'll fall behind and stop coming like you did before."

Peridot laughed, though it sounded forced, even to her. "How does anyone get anything done if they're in lessons for half of every day?"

"You'll still have plenty of time to hunt and watch your dragons and wolves. We're always out by midday."

"Has it gotten any more interesting? I always get so bored."

"That's because you weren't paying attention. It's interesting if you decide you want to learn."

Peridot smiled weakly and changed the subject. "Do you think my brother's all right? I don't have a clue where he's gone. I hope nothing happened. If he's gotten hurt or something, it's my fault."

"How would he get hurt? He was just going to your garden, right?"

"Yeah, but he wasn't there, was he?" Peridot shrugged and continued. "I don't know. Something feels off. Like something's messing with the mountain's energy. You don't feel it? Like an itch between your shoulder blades that won't go away?"

Bryoni looked at her as if she'd lost her mind. "You're starting to sound like you *have* gone a bit off. What could possibly upset a mountain? It's a pile of rocks and trees and minerals."

Peridot laughed again, but this time it was genuine. "You know what I mean. Our powers come from the mountain, right?"

Bryoni nodded.

"So, we have to stay in touch with the mountain if we want to use our powers. It's not difficult. It changes with the weather and seasons, but something feels wrong right now. I felt it when I was up there today. All the animals are on edge. Even the dragons are acting weird."

Bryoni made a face.

"What? Come with me tomorrow. I'll show you." Peridot grinned and started planning their trek up to the ruined city.

"Don't you have to get ready for your special guests tomorrow?"

"Well, yes, but I'll have time to go up to the ruins for a bit in the morning. We just won't be able to stay long. Come with me. We'll leave with the sunrise so there's plenty of time to get back and help Mother prepare for Lord Maksym's special visit." She made a gagging noise, and both dissolved in giggles.

Bryoni frowned. "I thought they were supposed to arrive today, but I haven't seen the carriage come through. Maybe they got delayed."

"Who cares? Angene's been insufferable since they set up this meeting. If they never show up, I wouldn't be upset."

Neither spoke for a long while, and Bryoni sighed. "Fine. I'll go with you. But you have to promise to come to lessons for a week."

"All right." Peridot forced an exaggerated sigh. "I'll go. Every single day. For a whole week." She groaned and fell back against the soft bearskin.

Bryoni slapped her shoulder and laughed. "It's not that bad, I promise."

They said their good nights and planned to meet at Peridot's garden gate at sunrise, and Peridot headed back out into the wind which had picked back up while she'd been inside. A light rain pelted her face, stinging like a hundred bees with the force of the wind. She hoped Kent had made it home. He didn't know where any of the best places were to get out of weather like this.

SUNRISE

*P*eridot woke to a crushing silence before the sun rose. She lay still in the darkness and listened to Angene's soft snores and focused on finding whatever sound had woken her. Nothing. Careful not to make any noise, she stretched and rolled out of bed. She'd set out her day clothes in the dressing room, so she slipped quietly through the curtain to dress. On the way, she peeked into Kent's room to see if he'd made it home, but his bed was empty and neatly made. She'd tell Bryoni they had to find him first, then they could all go up to the ruins together.

In the main room, she shoved her water cannister, two apples, a handful of deer jerky, and several leftover rolls into a bag, grabbed her old bow and quiver, and headed out into the early spring morning. A thin layer of frost covered the ground, and Peridot cursed. That would kill all the berries in the garden and put her mother in a foul temper to start the day. She breathed a sigh of relief that she wouldn't have to hear it. At least she had thought to put on her wool knickers and undershirt under her leather hunting clothes, so she'd be warm enough on the mountain. The black leather shirt and pants had protected her from falls through the years, but they rubbed uncomfortably against her still-tender knees and elbows.

The mountain's lights shone brilliantly over the town, drowning out the dawn's more muted blush. Streaks of blue, green, and purple light hovered above the rooftops, close enough Peridot almost thought she could reach up and touch them. She smiled. The lights low to the ground meant her powers would be stronger today.

"You look in a better mood this morning."

Peridot jumped and spun to face Bryoni, who wore two heavy cloaks over her tawny leather pants and shirt. She had her hands stuffed in a heavy wool muff. "Are you sure you'll be warm enough? Will you be able to keep up in all that?"

Bryoni chuckled. "I don't know how you don't freeze out here. I get so cold."

"We'll be moving, so that'll help you keep warm. We need to look for Kent, though. He didn't make it home last night."

A worried look creased Bryoni's features. "Where do you think he went? He's strong enough to look after himself, don't you think?"

"Strong enough? Definitely. He's just not good at watching his back. Remember when that cougar almost dragged him off when he was aiming for the elk? He gets too focused on what's in front of him. It leaves him open to attack from any other direction."

"Right. Good point. So where do we look first?"

Bryoni made a face that could have been a forced smile but looked closer to a grimace.

Peridot pointed toward the back of the garden. "We'll look for prints back there, since he said he was starting in the garden."

They set off and spent half an hour searching for footprints or any sign that he'd been in the garden. Finally, Peridot found a deep impression behind one of the overgrown blueberry bushes.

"Here," she called to Bryoni, who hurried over to her. "This is going to be harder because of all that rain. At least we know he was here. It looks like he may have slipped here. Let's follow it out a bit and see if we can find another."

Several paces away, another deep print marred the earth, followed by another a few steps away. One more slid under the garden gate, and Peridot swung it open and continued the search. They found two more prints on the trail leading to the mountain. After that, the prints disappeared into the tall grass surrounding the village.

"Well, we'll assume he kept moving in the same direction," Peridot said. "But we'll go slow and watch for signs that he turned."

The sun crept further into the sky while they searched, but they found no sign of Kent between the village and the outer trees that marked the edge of the mountain's forest. There, they stopped to rest on a downed tree. Peridot pulled out two of the rolls and her water cannister.

"I'm embarrassed I didn't think to bring water or anything," Bryoni said after a long drink. "I didn't think we'd need it since we need to be back by lunch."

"That's all right. I brought enough for us both."

They ate their snack in silence and packed the rest of the water away for later.

"All right. Which way from here?" Bryoni surveyed the landscape with her hands on her hips.

"Let's look for prints again. The trees may have protected them from the rain a bit."

They walked in a slow circle around the area, searching for any sign of Peridot's brother.

"What's this?" Bryoni pointed at the ground beside a large tree.

Peridot hurried over to her friend. A deep indentation marked the ground where she pointed, but it was far too big to be from Kent's foot.

"I don't know. That isn't Kent's footprint, but it's fresh. Let's see if there's any more."

They spread their circle out by ten paces and picked up a trail.

"It isn't Kent, but we'll follow it and see if it leads us to him. It's definitely a sprite, but I don't know who could have made it."

"What if it's the old man from the stories? They say he's dangerous." Bryoni hugged her muff close to her chest and glanced around as if something was about to jump out of the bushes at her.

Peridot shook her head dismissively. "I'm not worried about stories and legends. I've spent years up here and never saw him. Let's deal with what's in front of us, okay?"

They followed the trail quietly for over an hour. It led them over boulders and downed trees, across a stream, and higher into the mountains. It avoided the well-traveled path but stayed twenty paces to its right, which concerned Peridot. She didn't know anyone who wouldn't keep to the trail.

When they rounded a curve, Peridot froze. Something red and raw lay in the path. It wasn't moving, but terror filled her and locked her joints in place. Beside her, Bryoni gagged.

"What is that?" Bryoni whispered.

Peridot shook her head, unable to speak. Instead, she forced her legs into motion and stepped close to investigate.

"Oh, no," she moaned, dropping to her knees as realization struck. "It's one of the wolves. Who could have done this? Why? Why kill something and leave it to rot like this?"

Tears choked her, and she sobbed quietly for a long while.

"Uh, Peridot?" The sadness and horror in Bryoni's voice echoed that coursing through Peridot. "I think you'd better have a look at this."

Peridot peeled her eyes off the mangled carcass in front of her and followed Bryoni's voice. There, thirty paces further into the forest, lay another red lump.

"Oh, no. How many? I can't..." Grief shook her shoulders as she wondered how many of her beloved pack had fallen in the night. Without their coats and heads, she couldn't even identify the animals.

"I see three," Bryoni whispered.

Peridot let out a loud sob and clamped a hand over her mouth. Whoever killed those wolves might still be nearby.

"I'm sorry. I know you love them, but should we stay here? Everyone knows it's against the law to kill the wolves, so this could be someone dangerous. Do you think it's the old man? They say he has no concern for sprites' laws."

Peridot sniffled and stood. "No, we need to keep moving. Whoever did this couldn't have gotten far. And stop worrying about the stories. They're just myths told to frighten children away from the mountain." *I hope.* She didn't say the last bit aloud for fear it would only scare Bryoni more.

She hoped Kent hadn't run into whoever had killed the wolves. If he had, he could be in grave danger--or worse.

Pushing that thought out of her mind, she turned her face away from the dead wolves. Birds chirped in the tree-tops, the cheerful sound grating on Peridot's raw nerves. She wanted to scream at them but bit her tongue. She couldn't announce her presence, not when someone so dangerous could be nearby.

"I can't just leave them," she whispered to Bryoni. "Help me bury them, at least. We could use your sword to dig." She thought for a long moment. "We'll have to take turns, since I don't have a sword. My arrows won't help any." Peridot suddenly wished she had a blade in case they had to fight. Arrows were great at a distance, but useless in close combat.

Bryoni shook her head. "The sword won't help, either. Digging will ruin it, and we might need it later. Hold this and cover me." Bryoni handed her the sword and pushed up her pale leather sleeves.

"Excavo," Bryoni breathed. A soft yellow light flowed through her hands. The earth moved aside and opened a deep hole in front of the closest carcass.

The two worked together and moved the dead wolf

into the hole, then Bryoni uttered another charm and covered it with the loose soil. They repeated the process for the other two wolves. By the time the last wolf was covered, a sheen of sweat shone on Bryoni's face. Peridot waited while she drank from the water canister. As soon as she'd finished, they set out in search of Kent.

Peridot worked to curb her sobbing and sniffling, but she couldn't push the image of those mangled corpses out of her mind. Bryoni patted her arm and watched with sympathetic eyes, but she couldn't understand. To Bryoni, they had been dangerous wild animals. To Peridot, they'd been friends.

The niggling worry in the back of her mind wouldn't be ignored for long, though. Why hadn't they seen any sign of Kent? Fear opened a pit in Peridot's stomach. What if he'd met the same fate as the wolves?

Somewhere nearby, a twig snapped. Peridot froze and pressed herself up against a broad tree. Bryoni mirrored Peridot's response.

Peridot stood immobile, the tree's bark biting into the back of her head as she listened to the sounds of the forest. The birds and squirrels continued their cheerful symphony above, punctuated by the rustling of the leaves in the cold wind. She couldn't pick out any other sounds of movement. She waited several minutes, barely daring to breathe, before stepping away from the tree and taking stock of her surroundings.

Across the small clearing, something dark fluttered in the wind. Peridot stayed perfectly still and watched, but whatever it was didn't move from its spot on a low branch. She crept across the soft ground and chuckled softly. She grabbed her cloak and stuffed it into her pack, then turned her attention back to the forest.

Try as she might, she couldn't see anything out of place. She gestured for Bryoni, and the friends continued to follow the unusual tracks deeper into the forest.

POACHERS

They crept along for most of the morning, following the trail. It doubled back on itself several times. Frustration grew alongside the grief in Peridot's chest as they followed the tracks around a small copse of trees. They were wasting their time. She just knew it. She glanced up at the sun, almost at its zenith, and pushed the mental image of her angry mother out of her mind. She kept her mind blank and continued to follow the large divots.

Noon came and went. They'd been walking for hours when a second set of tracks met the ones they'd been following. The wind whistled through the branches above, drowning out Peridot's cry of surprise. She waved Bryoni over to where she stood.

Neither spoke, but Peridot hoped Bryoni understood the danger of their situation. Silently, Peridot pulled out her bow. She nocked an arrow and held it low, ready to draw and shoot if needed. Bryoni pulled both her long, thin sword and dagger and held them ready. Wary, but prepared, the two women moved forward. Peridot tried to keep behind the trees for cover and moved quickly from one broad trunk to the next.

Several quiet, tense minutes passed before Peridot heard voices on the wind. She couldn't make out words, but at least three distinct voices spoke in turn and over each other. She slowed her pace, checking around each tree before proceeding onward, crawling from tree to tree to keep herself hidden in the underbrush, and watching where she set her hands and feet to avoid any noise that would give away her position. Bryoni copied her movements, though her weapons got in the way and snagged on underbrush. After the first three paces, Bryoni sheathed her sword and just kept her dagger out.

As they moved uphill, the voices grew louder and more raucous. Bursts of coarse laughter punctuated the conversation. The scents of woodsmoke and cooking meat made Peridot's stomach grumble, but she ignored her hunger and pressed onward. Finally, they reached the edge of a small clearing. Peridot hid behind a broad juniper tree and peered into the clearing through the feathery branches.

Three burly men sat around a campfire. They were taller than any sprite Peridot had ever seen, maybe tall enough to climb the stairs in the ruins without straining. Three similarly tall women tended the fire and served meat and drinks to the men. The wolves' skins had been stretched between sticks set into the ground to dry by the fire.

Peridot's vision went red at the sight of her beloved friends' skins. She recognized one as the same wolf she'd healed only the day before. She stared for a long while before tearing her eyes away from the gruesome sight and scanning the rest of the camp. Three faded canvas tents sat next to each other on the north end of the clearing, fifty paces from the fire. Beside the first tent, something moved in the shadows of an enormous fir tree. Peridot squinted and leaned forward for a better look.

Tattered, dirty, and bleeding from an injury on his arm and a scrape on his cheek, her brother leaned against the tree and spat into the bushes. Peridot stifled a gasp. How had they captured Kent? A soft cry beside her betrayed Bryoni's emotion.

Her mind spun, but Peridot refused to rush into a situation like this. She signaled to Bryoni, and the two backed away from the camp without a sound.

When they'd put several dozen paces between themselves and the men, she spun and faced Bryoni. "What do we do? How do we get him free?" She kept her voice to a whisper but couldn't hide her fear.

Bryoni's wide, terrified eyes held no answers. She merely shook her head.

"Well, we can't just leave him. You saw what they did to the wolves. What if they try to do something similar to Kent?"

"Don't be ridiculous," Bryoni whispered. "Why would they try to skin your brother?"

"I don't know. I can't think! Where do you think they came from?" Peridot racked her mind for anything she could use to free her brother.

"I don't know..." Bryoni trailed off and stared toward the camp.

"How are we going to get him free?"

They spent well over an hour developing and

discarding ideas and crept back to the camp no more prepared than when they'd crawled away. The afternoon light faded into evening, and Peridot hoped she could find a way to free her brother and get home before dark.

They watched from the bushes while the men and women in the camp ate their dinner.

"We should give him some," the tallest man said, hitching a thumb toward Kent. "He'll need 'is strength if 'e's going to make it back to Tillamook. Should fetch a good price, though. He's strong enough for 'is kind."

"What about the other one?"

Peridot's head jerked toward the woman who spoke. *Other one?*

The first man laughed, and the cold sound of it sent a chill up Peridot's spine. "If it's awake, give it something to eat. Maybe we can get it strong enough to take with us."

Frantic, Peridot scanned the camp again, more slowly. This time, she saw something lying motionless under a tree opposite Kent.

"Who is it?" Bryoni whispered in Peridot's ear.

"I don't know. I can't tell from here." Peridot stood still, considering their options. "What if I make a noise and distract them, and you circle around to see who it is?"

"Distract them how?"

Peridot held up a hand in a gesture that imitated her using her powers.

"Are you sure? Have you practiced enough? I can do it if you're not sure." The doubt on Bryoni's face grated against Peridot's raw nerves.

Peridot pressed her lips in a line and nodded. "I can manage."

Without another word, Bryoni tiptoed back into the

forest where she could sneak toward the unmoving prisoner without the poachers seeing her.

Peridot waited, watching for some sign that Bryoni had made it to the unknown prisoner.

"—gonna make quite a payload. Think we'll get us a dragon? Or even better, an egg?"

The men's conversation drew her attention, though she didn't take her eyes from the tree line.

"How you think we'll manage that? You see how big those things are?"

"Don't be stupid," a woman cut in. "You take on those flying beasts, and you'll be their dinner. The man said they can blow fire, so they'll cook you before they eat you."

The men laughed, and one grabbed at the woman's dress. She swatted him away, and they laughed again.

A light flashed in the bushes behind the prisoner, though it vanished as quickly as it appeared. Peridot peered into the shadows until she could make out Bryoni's tawny leather shirt.

Peridot raised her hand and breathed in, pulling the mountain's power in through her hand-sewn leather shoes and filling her chest with its raging heat. The power both thrilled and frightened her, but she worked to keep her mind on the task at hand.

She focused hard on a point to her left, away from both Bryoni and Kent, and whispered a charm. Blue light engulfed her hands, but instead of going where she wanted, it flew off behind her and exploded. The wave of power knocked her to her knees and lit up the darkening sky.

Cursing under her breath, she leapt to her feet and ran

left, trying to circle around away from the explosion before the people in the camp went to investigate.

"What was that?"

"Let's go!"

"We've been found!"

The men and women in the camp all exclaimed at once, and the noise of boots stomping through the forest carried over the roaring of the mountain-powered blaze. Peridot hoped she hadn't injured any birds or small animals with that explosion, though she knew it was unlikely it had landed somewhere completely free of wildlife.

Peridot sprinted around and stopped at the edge of the clearing to watch the men and women fan out in the direction of the explosion. When the last one slipped into the forest, she took a deep breath and dashed through the camp toward her brother.

He sat with his back to the tree, watching the commotion, and his mouth dropped open when he spotted her. "Peri!" He whispered when she reached him. "What are you doing? You have to get out of here." The fear and relief in his wide eyes cemented her resolve.

Peridot didn't answer. Instead, she pulled her belt knife and cut the ropes that bound him to the tree. "Let's go." She pulled him up and into the woods behind the tent.

When she didn't head toward home, he stopped and pointed in the correct direction. She shook her head and continued around the camp.

"Hey! The prisoners!" A deep voice jump-started Peridot's heart.

"Run!" She whispered, but instead of moving toward

the safety of home, she led him through the forest toward the spot where she'd last seen Bryoni.

Every few steps, she turned to make sure the poachers hadn't spotted them. She nocked an arrow and held it against her bowstring, ready to shoot at a moment's notice.

They kept to the shadows as they rounded the tents and ran straight into Bryoni, who stepped out from behind a tree at their approach.

"Who is it?" Peridot asked, breathless.

"I don't know, but he's on his feet." She pointed back toward the tree she'd been hiding behind. "I don't think he'll be able to keep up for long. Let's go."

"Kent, do you think you can help him?" She waited until her brother had an arm around the stranger. "This way." Peridot stepped deeper into the forest, anxious to get away from the encampment.

She weaved her way up the steep hillside, keeping well away from the game trails and hunters' paths that wound through that area. If she had been alone, Peridot would have run, but the second prisoner staggered and wobbled on his feet and needed help from at least two of them to climb over the downed trees and boulders blocking their path.

FREEDOM

"*W*ait. I-I can't...I need a break," the wounded man they'd freed gasped after an hour of frantic hiking and climbing.

Peridot led the group to a shallow crevice in the mountainside and helped the injured man down. She pulled the last of her bread and water from her pack and split the bread into four pieces. She handed the water canister to the injured man and let him have his fill, then refilled it from the shallow stream running through the little gulch.

Peridot, Kent, and Bryoni knelt on the pebbled banks and scooped water into their hands to drink. When they'd slaked their thirst, all four sprites leaned back against the ice-cold vertical wall protecting their hiding place. Kent and the prisoner shivered in their thin clothes.

"Here." Peridot pulled her cloak out of her pack and wrapped it around Kent. "Bryoni, can he use one of your cloaks?"

Bryoni didn't answer but pulled off the top cloak and handed it to the wounded man. He struggled to wrap it around his shoulders, so Peridot helped him and clasped it at his throat.

Peridot listened to the forest, searching for any sound that didn't fit the mountain's pattern, any sign that the poachers had tracked them. Only the sounds of the forest answered back: the chirping of birds, squirrels chattering, the leaves rustling in the evening wind.

Satisfied, Peridot turned to get a better look at the man they'd rescued. She was certain she'd never seen him before, though his left eye was swollen shut and surrounded by angry-looking bruises and his lips were swollen to twice their normal size.

"What's your name?" She whispered.

"Simran." He winced as if the name hurt to pronounce, and fresh blood beaded at the corner of his mouth.

"I'm Peridot, and this is Bryoni and Kent. We'll get to know each other a bit better when we're safe." A gust of cold wind whistled through the gulley, and she glanced up at the treetops whipping side to side. Peridot shivered and pulled her cloak closer. "We need to get out of the forest before that wind gets any stronger."

Kent frowned and stared up into the sky. "How are we supposed to get out of the forest before dark? It's nearly sunset already. Mother will be worried sick."

A bitter laugh escaped from Peridot's lips. "More like she'll be angry we haven't given her something special to serve her guests tonight. I wonder how Angene will handle *that* predicament."

"Don't be that way," Kent chided. "They just want to get off to the right start with Lord Maksym's nephew."

"Right. And they want to get me married to the ancient Lord Maksym as soon as possible." She shuddered.

Simran groaned and dropped his battered head into his hands.

"What's wrong? Does it hurt?" Bryoni scooted closer and pressed a hand to his shoulder. "We'll get you healed up once we find some decent cover."

He didn't answer, but Peridot stood and lifted her pack off the muddy ground. "We'd better get moving. I think we lost them for a bit, but they'll find our tracks soon enough."

Bryoni and Kent stood and brushed themselves off, but Simran didn't move. Peridot stepped over to him and prodded him gently. "Do you think you can go on? It's not much farther to the ruins, and I know a good place we can hide for the night."

Simran nodded and held out his arms so Kent and Peridot could help him up. He stumbled a bit but steadied himself against a tree trunk and pulled his arms free. "Let's go."

Peridot stayed close enough to the stream that the stones would hide their tracks but far enough away that her feet didn't get wet. The others stayed right on her heels. They stayed in the crevice until it leveled out with the forest around them. A dozen paces later, the stream narrowed enough that they could easily leap across. Peridot and Kent helped Simran over. The burbling sound of water rounding the bend should have been enough to cover the sound of their retreat, so Peridot urged them faster down into the valley below the ruined city.

They'd only walked for ten minutes past the stream

when Simran tripped over a stone and fell face-first into a bramble bush. The crash and moans that followed set Peridot's heart racing. She helped Kent and Bryoni pull the injured man back out of the bushes and waited to see if the poachers had been within hearing distance. Somewhere nearby, a man's voice called out, followed by a series of answering shouts.

Peridot cursed and looped an arm under Simran's shoulder. Kent took the other side and they half-carried, half-dragged the injured man down the hillside. He was heavier than she'd expected, and within twenty paces, Peridot was gasping for breath.

"There they are!" A man yelled close behind them.

The shout turned Peridot's legs to jelly, but she ran faster. Simran had gone limp, so she dragged his arm further over her shoulders and held on as tight as she could.

"Let me have him," Bryoni said, running beside Peridot.

Peridot frowned, unable to hide her confusion. "We can't stop here."

"No, not stop. You can shoot," Bryoni said between gasping breaths.

"Oh, right."

Peridot slowed her steps and ducked out from under Simran's heavy arm. Without stopping, the women switched places. As soon as she was free, Peridot pulled her bow off her back, yanked an arrow from her quiver, nocked it, and turned. She loosed three arrows in rapid succession without turning back toward the ruins. All three hit their mark, and the largest of their pursuers fell. One fletching stuck out of his chest.

It must have hit a rib, Peridot thought.

Two patches of blood stained his shirt where the other arrows had passed straight through him.

Something caught her foot as she ran, and Peridot stumbled. She spun, pitched forward, and couldn't help falling on her face on the uneven ground. A rock caught her in the chest and knocked the wind out of her. She lay there, immobile for several seconds and pressed herself up from the ground as soon as she could breathe. The poachers were only a few feet away from her. Desperate, she raised both hands, breathed in the mountain's power, and focused on her enemies.

She waited until the energy in her chest made it hard to draw a breath and whispered, "Impello."

Blinding yellow light shot out of her hands and enveloped the men and women running toward her.

Peridot cursed. The light should have been blue if she'd gotten the charm right. The ball of light lifted the poachers off the ground and held them captive there, but it wouldn't last long. She'd only suspended them instead of knocking them back.

She didn't wait to see how long it would hold. Instead, she turned and sprinted toward the knee-height stairs where her friends struggled to get Simran up each level.

When she reached them, she finally dared to look back. The poachers still hovered above the ground, but the light had faded to a dim haze and they dropped closer to the grass with every passing second.

"Let's go! Simran, you have to help us."

The injured man raised his head and glanced around. A flash of fear shone in his eyes, and he straightened his back.

Peridot smiled and tried to make her voice sound encouraging. "That's it. Raise your leg. We have to get into the city before they get here, or we won't stand a chance."

The sweat rolling down Kent's face worried her, but she didn't comment. Instead, she scrambled to the top of the stairs and raised her bow. She nocked an arrow, took aim, and let the arrow fly. It struck the front poacher above the knee. He screamed and stumbled but stayed on his feet for a few steps. She loosed another arrow that took him in the shoulder, and he screamed again and fell. She didn't even care that he wasn't dead--in fact, it made her feel a tiny bit better to stop him without killing him. She nocked another arrow and focused on the woman sprinting down the hill.

"Let's go! We're up!" Kent's voice interrupted her aim, and the arrow flew wild.

Peridot spun and moved to take Bryoni's spot under Simran's left arm. Now that he was awake, he helped by keeping his legs beneath him and supporting most of his weight, so they moved at a pace that she'd almost call a jog.

"This way! Bryoni, make sure they don't sneak up behind us. We need to get out of sight."

Peridot grabbed her brother's free arm and pulled him to the left, toward a narrow opening between two fallen pillars.

"Through here! Quick!" She pulled and heaved until Simran and Kent were through the opening and turned back to Bryoni. "Put some of the stones over our tracks. Make sure they can't tell we came this way."

Bryoni didn't bend down. Instead of moving the

stones by hand, as Peridot expected, she raised her hands and the pebbles along their entire path through the city shifted, covering any tracks they'd left.

"I really need to practice more," Peridot muttered low enough the others couldn't hear.

ESCAPE

"Keep moving," Peridot warned as soon as Bryoni had finished. "But be careful. This part of the city is crumbling."

Kent frowned and examined the decaying stone wall beside him. "What part isn't? How much farther is it? I don't think we can go much further."

"We can't stop yet." Peridot stared off into the dim alleyway. "We have to get down into the caves. It's not much farther, I swear."

Kent grunted but didn't say anything else, so Peridot set off down the treacherous path. The wide paving stones beneath her feet had crumbled to a fine gravel which crunched and shifted with every step. Stone half-walls bordered the alley on both sides, the sad remains of what must have been grandiose buildings in their prime. Ancient people had carved foreign symbols into some of the stones, but Peridot had no idea what they said. Only the best scholars in the village could read the giants' scripts, and she hadn't studied anywhere near enough to be able to join them.

At the bottom of the steep decline, she stopped and glanced around, searching for landmarks to get her bearings. She didn't normally reach the caves this way, but it was the best route for staying out of sight. "This way," she said, guiding Simran to the right and around another corner. "We're almost there."

The space between the walls narrowed, and the light faded, blocked by loose stones that had fallen over the top of the alley and rested on the two crumbling walls on either side. Peridot stopped and waited for her eyes to adjust. She moved slower once she could see. The larger stones and pebbles underfoot shifted, and she worried she'd drop Simran or worse, turn an ankle or break her leg on the unstable ground. Ten more paces and relief flooded her when she saw what she'd been looking for: an opening the size of a small fireplace in the bottom of the stone wall.

"In here." She let go of Simran's arm and dropped to a crouch. When she'd slipped through the small opening, she dropped about four feet to the soft, sandy ground below. She held a hand up for the next person. Bryoni lowered her feet into the hole and dropped silently beside her.

"Simran next. We'll help him down," Peridot whispered, holding her hands out of the opening.

Kent helped the injured man to sit and hang his feet through the hole. He leaned back, and Peridot and Bryoni tugged on his legs until he slumped through the hole and fell on top of them. Peridot grunted, but Bryoni muttered something, and a green light erupted from her hands. It eased Simran off them and to a seated position against the wall, and Peridot turned back to the alley.

"Your turn," she called to her brother.

He hopped down without any fanfare and stood blinking beside her. Above them, someone shouted, and Peridot flinched.

"Can you cover our tracks again?" Peridot whispered to Bryoni.

Even before she'd finished speaking, Bryoni raised her hands and murmured a command. Soft purple light filled the cavern and, just like before, the pebbles and stones shifted to hide their tracks. When the light died off, Peridot grabbed Simran's arm and pulled him to his feet.

"Just a little further," she reassured him. He groaned and wobbled but stayed upright. Kent positioned himself beside the wounded man once more and supported him as he staggered along behind Peridot.

Unbothered by the close confines of the caves, Peridot led the group through the growing darkness. She moved with confidence, though she felt more unsure than she wanted her friends to know. She hoped she wasn't leading them all to their deaths.

"Are you sure this is the right way?" Bryoni asked after several long minutes of walking in silence. "I can't see anything."

"Yes, you can. It's not completely dark. Look, there are openings in the stone above us. They let in enough light to see where we're going." Peridot waved her hand between the light and Bryoni's face, using the shadow to illustrate her point.

No one spoke, and Peridot listened to her friends' even breathing and soft crunch of footsteps as they worked their way deeper into the cave system that connected the ruins to the mines below.

After another fifteen minutes of walking, they reached a cavern with no light. Bryoni held out a palm and ignited a tiny white light, just enough to see their surroundings.

"This will do," Peridot said. "Here, sit down. Let's get those wounds healed."

She knelt beside a soft patch of dirt and waited for Simran to comply. He didn't. Instead, he looked to Kent with a worried expression.

"Just do what she says." Kent sounded exasperated and exhausted. "She's the best healer we've got. You won't be able to keep going much longer in your condition."

The injured man swayed and dropped to his knees. He paused there for a breath and lowered himself to sit in front of her.

A heavy silence filled the cavern, punctuated by the soft rustling of cloth as Kent and Bryoni settled down to watch and rest. The soft light flickered and shifted when Bryoni sat, but she kept it going. Peridot gulped and focused on the mountain surrounding her. She needed to borrow its energy and had no room for mistakes. If she got the charm wrong, as she had with the wolves, she feared she'd lose not only Simran's trust, but Kent's and Bryoni's, too.

Faint light filtered in through the corridor they'd traversed, complimenting the light Bryoni cast from her hands. The soft breathing of her friends echoed in the cramped space. Somewhere in the distance, water trickled through a system of underground streams, pressing its way down the inside of the mountain.

Peridot closed her eyes and pulled the mountain's

energy into her chest. When the wild, uncontrollable pressure built to an unbearable level, she drew a shallow breath and held out one finger. "Integro," she whispered. Her legs trembled with the force of the command's energy. Her arm felt heavy and weak, but she worked to hold it steady.

A soft green light enveloped her hand. She touched Simran's face, running her finger over his injured eye and down to his bruised and swollen lips. A jolt of energy shot through her arm and increased her pulse, but she ignored it and focused on sending the mountain's healing power into the man in front of her. She watched, transfixed, as her fingers trailed over his face, leaving a path of fading bruises and mending skin. The light grew to a bold emerald, and she raised her eyes from his face to make sure the glow wouldn't draw their pursuers' attention. She thought she'd chosen their location well, though, and no openings in the cave showed her light from the outdoors. They should be safe enough to continue.

She returned her fingers to his jaw, tracing the stubble-rough skin and searching for any injuries. Simran gasped, and Peridot hoped he felt a tiny bit of the excitement coursing through her at the feel of his skin beneath her fingers. She felt along the other side of his jaw, mending a small break she detected there, and stopped, her hand hovering an inch from his chest.

"Where else are you hurt?"

"My… My arm." He held up his right arm, which hung oddly from the elbow.

It must have worsened from being used to support his weight down the hills. Peridot didn't remember it being so misshapen outside the camp. She pressed the first two fingers of her right hand to the break and held them there, watching as the green light flowed from her hand and into his arm. He gasped and cried out as the bones snapped back into place.

"Hush. You have to keep quiet." Peridot spoke gently, as if reassuring an injured child, but her heart fluttered and raced at the muscular strength in his arms. "Where else?"

Simran drew an unsteady breath and pointed to the lower ribs on his right side.

"You might want to lie down. This one may hurt a bit more." Peridot grimaced and wished she knew the charms to numb the areas being healed. Broken ribs were extremely painful.

Silently, Simran eased himself onto his back in the sand.

Peridot felt along his chest for the injured ribs and repeated the charm, letting the light flow from herself and into him. The bones snapped and popped as they reset and knit themselves, but some deeper injury pulled her to it. She drew a deep breath and pressed her palm against his abdomen, feeling the strength of the muscles there but focusing her energy on what lay beneath them. Sweat beaded on her brow, and she narrowed her eyes, blocking everything but his blood-stained shirt from her view.

"There," She whispered, feeling the broken vessels starting to weave their way back to their severed ends.

Simran gasped and writhed, but she kept her hand firmly pressed against his abdomen. There were so many injuries. Too many. Every time she healed one, another attracted the energy. The light inside her started to fade, so she released him and closed her eyes. Sweat dripped down her back from the effort. She drew several deep, cleansing breaths, pulling energy up through her feet and into her chest. Replenished, she set her hand lightly on his stomach, stroking side to side across his abdomen and healing the bruises and wounds beneath the surface.

When she could find no further injuries, she opened her eyes and met his gaze. "How are your legs?"

He gulped and his throat worked as he fought to push the words out. "The right one."

Peridot nodded and pressed both hands to his ankle. A deep cut in his calf had been unwashed for too long, and infection swelled everything below the knee. It took several minutes of deep concentration to push the infection out and close the wound. She worked her way up his leg and stopped with her hand on his hip, feeling the bones there shifting into proper alignment.

"Any other injuries?" She asked when the energy stopped flowing. She set her hand on his chest and tried to focus, searching his aura for signs of injury.

He grabbed her hand and pressed it closer. His heart beat against her hand, strong and steady. Electricity shot through her when she met his eyes. His eyes widened, and he ran his tongue over his newly-healed lips.

"I don't think so. I'm just so tired." Simran dropped his head into the dirt and closed his eyes.

Peridot pulled her hand free. "I know. That's to be expected. We can't stay here, though. Do you think you can walk a little further?"

Simran drew a deep breath and held it, and Peridot guessed he was testing his ribs. He flexed his arms and legs and pressed his fingers against his jaw. "I think so. Help me up."

Kent and Bryoni each grabbed a hand and pulled him to his feet while Peridot struggled to stand up beside him. Weariness shook her knees and robbed her of breath, but she pushed herself upright. They couldn't stay in the cavern. For one, it would be too easy for their pursuers to find. Besides that, the temperature had dropped even in the few minutes they'd spent there, and Peridot's breath puffed out in clouds in front of her. They had to find someplace warm to sleep, or they'd freeze.

"It's not much farther," Peridot whispered, reassuring herself along with everyone else. "Bryoni, can you cover us again? Make sure they can't follow our tracks?"

Bryoni nodded. All four sprites moved to the end of the cave and waited while the sand and pebbles shifted to hide the blood stains and footprints that would betray them, though it was unlikely their pursuers would make it that far.

Peridot closed her eyes and listened to the mountain's sounds. The burbling of running water had grown louder. She focused on that sound and located it, off in the distance to her right.

"This way." She moved toward the water and trusted that the others would follow. Now that his wounds were healed, Simran should be able to make it the rest of the way, though the pain probably hadn't subsided yet.

The image of the mangled wolves flashed through her mind, and Peridot fought off a wave of grief. Those wolves were dead now, but she silently vowed that she'd die before she let their killers leave this mountain with their skins.

Perhaps, Peridot thought, she could somehow lure the poachers to the dragons' lair. If they got too close, the dragons would fight to defend their home, and they would win.

Holding her breath and listening to the water, she turned a corner to the left. Bright light nearly blinded her, and she stood frozen, waiting for her eyes to adjust. Behind her, three gasps echoed in the narrow stone corridor.

Peridot raised her eyes to the opening in the cave's roof and watched, transfixed, as four dragons swooped and dove into the forest nearby, their antics highlighted against a pink and orange-streaked sky.

"Here," she whispered, pressing back along the wall. "We can watch the dragons hunt while we wait for the poachers to give up and go back to their camp."

Simran shook his head but gaped at the dragons in clear view above them. "Can they see us?"

"I think so, but the opening's too small for them to reach us. I've spent hours here watching them." Peridot smiled and tried to identify the dragons, though it was impossible to tell their colors with the deepening twilight behind them.

Still smiling, Peridot leaned against the wall and let her knees go slack so she slid down to a sitting position. She patted the soft dirt beside her and waited. One by one, Kent, Bryoni, and Simran sat beside her, each staring up through the hole and watching the dragons' graceful ballet.

Brilliant streaks of color painted the deepening sky, and Peridot watched the colors sharpen and fade before she sighed and stood.

"The sun's setting. That means we're stuck in the mountains for the night. It's not wise to try to escape in the dark. Follow me. We need someplace warm to settle in, or we'll all freeze to death."

Somewhere above, close to the cave's roof, a twig snapped. Without a sound, Peridot ushered the others through the exposed cavern and into the safety of darkness on the other side. There, they stopped and watched the sky through the opening. Peridot held her breath. The crunching footsteps hadn't sounded like an animal.

A head appeared over the cavern, and the man cupped his hands over his eyes and peered down into the cave.

Peridot extended her arms and pressed her friends further into the darkness but kept a close watch on the man above them.

"Do you see anything? Are they down there?" A woman's shrill voice sounded from above.

"Something's been there, but it's probably more of those damn dogs," the man called back. "There's no sign of blood or nothing. That weakling sprite'll be trailing blood wherever he goes."

Simran tensed against Peridot's restraining arm, but he kept quiet. She guessed he probably didn't like being called a weakling. The muscles she'd felt beneath his clothes certainly hadn't been weak. Her pulse quickened at the memory, but she shoved the feelings aside.

Peridot stayed at the edge of the cavern until the man stood, dusted himself off, and strode out of sight. When no more sounds of boots tromping overhead reached her ears, and she was sure it was safe, she led the others deeper into the caves. They crept along the passages until they reached a broad opening.

A menacing growl greeted them, raising the little hairs on Peridot's arms. Kent, who had been staying so close she could feel his breath on her neck, stepped back away from the warning, but Peridot cooed softly.

"It's all right. It's just me. Who's a good baby?" A hulking beast stepped out of the shadow and pressed its head into her outstretched hand. A heartbeat later, a warm, wet tongue streaked up her face as a second wolf joined the welcome.

Peridot chuckled and pulled Kent forward. She helped him hold out a hand palm down, so the wolves could investigate his scent. Like they had with Peridot, the animals licked his face and hands, and she knew he'd been accepted.

Bryoni came next. "Are you sure this is safe?" Fear roughened her voice, but she held out a hand the way Peridot showed her.

"Safer than anywhere out there." Peridot gestured to the corridor they'd just left.

With a weak shrug, Bryoni stepped up beside Peridot and let the wolves sniff her. They accepted her instantly, licking her face and hands and nibbling at the tassels hanging from the front of her pale leather shirt.

When it was his turn, Simran hung back. "I don't think this is a good idea. I've never really been around animals," he whispered.

"Relax. Wolves are excellent judges of character, or so I've heard." She smiled at him, and he stepped forward, hesitant, but trusting.

A low warning growl echoed through the space. Peridot held up her hand to stop Simran but spoke softly to the wolves. "You're all right. He won't hurt you." She turned to Simran. "You probably smell like the poachers from being in their camp. Here, let me have your hand."

She grabbed his wrist and held his hand in both of hers, her arms extended to allow the wolves to smell his hand mingled with her scent.

This time, several wolves crowded around them, sniffing his hand and arm and making soft snuffling noises. Long, tense moments passed before one of them licked his fingers and pushed past her to lick at his face.

Simran sputtered and laughed but didn't pull away from the friendly beasts.

Once the wolves had accepted all of her group's members, Peridot led the others to a wide indentation in the western wall of the cavern.

AMBUSH

"We'll be safe here for the night," Peridot said, not bothering to whisper. She reasoned the wolves' shuffling and woofing would drown out any noise she made short of shouting.

"What makes you so sure?" Kent kept his voice low and seated himself beside her, but his back stayed rigid. "This looks like the opposite of safe to me."

Peridot smiled and waved a hand toward the two dozen wolves sitting and lying on the cavern's floor. "They've accepted you. All of you." She met Bryoni's eyes and Simran's before turning her attention back to Kent. "They won't turn on you now unless you threaten them."

"And how do I make sure they don't think I'm threatening?" Kent's fingers twitched near his belt, where his knife should have been, but the poachers had taken his weapons.

"Simple. Don't do anything to endanger them. As long as you settle down and rest, they'll protect you as one of their pack."

Bryoni sat and scooted until her back hit the stone wall. "Um, Peridot, I don't mean to be a downer, but weren't some of their pack killed by the poachers? What makes you think they can protect us?"

Tears welled in Peridot's eyes at the memory of the mangled carcasses and the skins stretched out near the poachers' fire. "Yes, but they were scouts. They would have been alone and easier to catch because they were patrolling their territory for any invaders, like other wolf packs. They've never had to watch out for poachers before. It's not unlikely that they got one, and the others came to help, and then they got the other two." She swiped at her eyes and dug in her pack for her water canister. "Regardless, you're safer here than you would be out in the forest overnight."

As if to verify her point, the wind outside the cave picked up, howling through the trees and hurling pinecones and twigs past the cavern's opening.

Peridot handed the water canister to Simran first. "Thirsty?"

He nodded and took the cool metal cylinder. He tipped it to his lips and took several long gulps before he lowered it and handed it to Bryoni.

"I don't have anything else to eat," Peridot said when they'd each had a good drink. She pushed the cork into the canister's top and dropped it back into her bag.

"We'll be all right until morning," Kent answered. "We've done without before."

Bryoni's stomach growled loudly as if to refute his claim.

"I'm sorry," Peridot said. "Will you be all right until morning? You're not used to missing meals, are you?"

"I'll be fine. I could stand to miss a meal or two." She patted her flat belly.

Peridot and Kent laughed along with her, but Simran had gone noticeably silent. Peridot glanced over to where he'd propped himself against the wall and laughed outright. He'd slumped over onto his side and fallen fast asleep. His mouth hung open, and a line of drool dripped into the sand. A soft snore escaped his open mouth.

"The poor dear," she murmured, pointing him out to her friends.

"Well, I've heard the healing charms exhaust the person being healed, so I'm sure he needs a good sleep to finish the job." Bryoni tucked her battered muff under his head and scooted back to the wall. She leaned her head back against the stone wall. "We should all probably follow his lead. Tomorrow's not likely to be any easier."

Peridot nodded but turned to her brother, her eyes bright with curiosity. "How *did* they catch you? I thought you were just going to the garden for the raccoons."

"I did. But something made a noise on the other side of the wall, and I went to check it out, in case it was a fox or something bigger." He paused and rubbed the back of his head. "When I opened the gate, something hit me hard on the back of the head, and I woke up in the camp with the poachers. I don't know how they managed to get that close without anyone seeing them, but then our house is on the very edge of town."

Peridot frowned. "How odd that they'd come so close to town either way. What would make them think they'd be safe there"

Kent laughed bitterly. "They're twice the size of anyone in town. Why wouldn't they be safe?"

"But wouldn't they know about our powers?" Bryoni asked. Her frown mirrored Peridot's confusion. "We've never had trouble from thieves or other criminals before because everyone from here to the plains knows we have the mountain's powers to protect us."

Peridot didn't have an answer to that, and apparently neither did Kent, since he just shook his head and didn't say anything.

Soon after that, they all lay down on the sandy cave floor to get some sleep. It had been a grueling day—for all of them—and they'd need their rest if they were going to outsmart the poachers and get home tomorrow. Peridot tucked her cloak around her and sighed. It wasn't long before oblivion took her.

PERIDOT WOKE before the sun and lay unmoving, listening for a repeat of the noise that had dragged her out of a sound sleep. The cold stone floor pressed into her cheek. Every muscle ached from the night spent with no cushion, but she didn't stretch, didn't move except the shallowest breaths she could manage.

There.

A branch snapped, followed by shuffling and sniffing noises. Something large moved at the mouth of the cave, but the wolves lay still and silent in the dark. Peridot wished she had the courage to sit up for a better view, but she didn't dare.

Focused on the individual sounds beyond the narrow opening, Peridot didn't see or hear the huge wolves crouched at the cave's mouth until they pounced.

The wolves snarled and snapped in unison, and the animal outside roared and screamed in pain for a breath before they silenced it forever.

Peridot sat up and stared into the darkened cave, straining her eyes to see what they'd caught. Her stomach grumbled at the thought of real food, but she didn't dare approach the wolves while they were eating. She'd spent enough time watching animals in the wild to know that the most dangerous animal is the one protecting his food or his babies. This cave now contained both. Peridot scooted until her back met the rough stone wall and watched the faint light at the cave's opening, uncertain what else she could safely do. While she waited for the wolves to finish their meal, her mind wandered over the predicament she and her friends were in. They had no food, and she was desperately short on arrows. Without both, they had no chance of making it safely out of the forest and back to the village.

If she could find a way to get to it, she had an old, handmade bow and full quiver in the remains of a building at the top of the hill, but there was no way to get there without going through the open courtyard at the center of the ruined city. That fact had never occurred to her before, but then she'd never had to worry about being spotted before, either.

Beside her, Bryoni groaned and sat up. "What's happening?" She rubbed at her eyes and squinted into the dark cave.

"The wolves caught something outside." Peridot whispered. "They're eating now. Just sit back and stay quiet. We don't want them to think we're a threat to their food."

Bryoni stretched and leaned back beside Peridot. Nearby, one of the men snored softly.

"So," Bryoni whispered. "What's the plan? I know you have something up your sleeve."

"Well..." Peridot hesitated a breath, then told Bryoni about the supplies stashed in the city. "I don't know how to get to them, though," she added.

The two talked softly, considering and discarding every idea they came up with, until daylight streamed through the cave's opening and Kent sat up and yawned. In the process, he bumped Simran, who groaned and stretched.

Peridot barely gave Simran time to lift his head before she started firing questions at him. "Good, you're awake. How do you feel? Are there any more injuries that we missed yesterday? Do you still hurt anywhere? I'm not sure I got all the injuries in your belly. Do you think you could eat?"

Simran sat up, groaned, and moved his arms and legs. "No, I think you fixed everything. And yes, I think for the first time in a week, I'm actually hungry. How'd you do that, anyway? That was pretty amazing." He pressed his fingers into his abdomen and Peridot tore her gaze away. Her fingers tingled at the memory of the taut muscles she'd felt there.

He grinned and his straight white teeth glistened in the morning sun. Peridot's heart skittered in her chest, which only irritated her. Her stomach grumbled. Hungry and annoyed, she scanned the wolves at the mouth of the cave. Most had finished eating and retreated to their den to clean themselves and sleep. Three or four wolves paced outside, protecting their kill from any scavengers in the area.

"What's your plan?" Kent echoed Bryoni's earlier question.

Peridot told the men about the bow and quiver in the city building. "What do you think? Do we go for it? I'm awfully low on arrows. How would we get to it?" she asked. "Or should we just leave it and try to get back to town?"

"Nah, we should get it. Two bows are better than one. What if we split up?" Kent suggested, keeping his eyes on the milling wolves. "Two of us can leave the cave and head toward the poachers' camp. That might pull anyone watching away from the cave, so you can get to the building and get the bow." He paused and glanced around. "Maybe we can meet back here in an hour or so?"

"That might work. How do we split up?" Peridot cocked her head and considered the group. "Kent, you know your way around this area as well as I do, so we should probably go separate ways. What about the others?"

"Well, I can go with Kent. I can do charms, and he can't, so I should be able to get us away safely if we get into trouble. You're good enough with the bow that I doubt you'll have any problems."

Peridot turned and met Simran's worried gaze. "What powers do you have?"

"I…I don't—Powers?" Simran sputtered. "I thought only the women here had powers."

"Don't worry about it." Peridot smiled. She hoped it looked reassuring. She didn't bother asking about weapons. He didn't have any. She would have found them if he had. She'd run her hands over most of his body during the healing session the night before. "Do you think you can keep up? Watch my back in case anyone sneaks up on us?"

"Yeah." Simran sounded relieved. "I can definitely do that much."

"Then it's settled." Someone's stomach growled, echoing the hunger in Peridot's belly. She raised her head and met each person's eyes. "We're not hunting. We're not looking for nuts or berries. We'll worry about food once we're properly armed."

"All right."

"Agreed."

"That's fair."

The voices blended so Peridot couldn't tell who said what, but it didn't matter. They agreed. Her heart sped up at the prospect of racing across the ruined city, exposed and unprotected, with poachers and slavers somewhere nearby. She considered the poachers' actions from the day before. They hadn't used any kind of powers, but that didn't mean they didn't have any. She'd have to be careful.

She closed her eyes and whispered a prayer, asking the mountain to protect her. She hoped none of the others heard her, since none of them practiced the old religion anymore. Peridot just hadn't been able to give it up. The new gods had never done anything for her, but the mountain was the source of her power and home to all her favorite creatures.

"All right, Let's get this started." Peridot stood and scratched the ear of the nearest wolf. "When you leave the cave, turn immediately so they know you're not going for their food."

Without another word, the four sprites moved quickly to the cave's exit, where they split and went in opposite directions. Kent and Bryoni exited first, stood tall, and strolled off toward their right. Peridot gave them several minutes as a head start, so anyone watching would follow them. When she could no longer make out the gleam of Kent's brilliant red hair against the deep green of the forest, Peridot stepped up to the cave's opening.

"Let's go." The words came out a breath above a whisper.

She didn't look back to see if Simran followed. Instead, she dashed to her left as fast as her legs would carry her. She sprinted past crumbling pillars standing as tall as two houses stacked atop one another, past a building that had only half fallen, whose stone walls still provided a modicum of protection to those creatures who found shelter in its impressive square. She raced past the marble statue that had fallen over a hundred years ago and been completely covered with moss and vines. At the orange-rusted remnants of an iron fence, she slowed.

Only a few more paces. There!

Peridot spun and dashed into a tiny shack pressed between two large stone structures. No door hung in the frame, but the slate roof had somehow survived the centuries of neglect. Inside, Peridot blinked and waited for her eyes to adjust to the dimness before she strode to the stone shelves lining the back wall. She'd heard a rumor that this had once been a wine cellar, but it served as a perfect place for her to store provisions for her long days on the mountain.

Excitement bubbled inside her chest as she reached up onto the highest shelf she could reach. Her fingers closed around the bow at the same time strong hands grabbed her waist from behind. Peridot froze as if waiting for a wild beast to pass or pounce. The warmth of his hands spread through her leather shirt, past her wool undergarments, and into her middle, lighting a fire inside that made her distinctly uncomfortable. He didn't release her.

"We have to get out of here and get help. We can't beat them." Simran murmured in her ear. "What's the fastest way back to your village?" He held her waist but didn't press closer.

Peridot grabbed the bow and the quiver's strap and lowered them to her side. She twisted, breaking his grip, and turned to face him. "I'm not leaving. My brother and my best friend are out there."

"You don't understand what you're up against. If they catch you, they'll kill you." He cursed. "They almost killed me. Would have, if it hadn't been for you."

"That's even more reason not to leave my family out here." Peridot pressed herself against the shelves and strained to see his face. "Look, I don't know you. You don't know me. I don't expect you to put your neck out for me. But I'm not leaving them out here. I'm going back."

"You can't! They'll expect that. They'll be waiting."

Peridot glared at him and pressed her palms against his linen-clad chest.

Linen? How'd he keep from freezing to death? She wondered distractedly. She gave a silent thanks for Bryoni's extra cloak, but that only explained how he'd survived last night. The previous weeks had been brutally cold at night, and some days hadn't been much warmer, even at high noon.

She dragged her thoughts back to the problem at hand. "The village is a straight shot that way." She pointed to her right, toward a narrow path. "When you meet the stream, follow it to the ledge, jump down, and it's just across the plain. I'm going back for my brother."

He leaned toward her, and she met his eyes, waiting. Electricity crackled in the air between them, but she held on tightly to her anger. When he closed his eyes and leaned close, she shoved at his chest with all she had. He stumbled backward and hit the stone wall. She sprinted for the door and out into the brilliant morning sun.

Her eyes stung and watered in the bright light, but Peridot didn't pause. Somewhere behind her, Simran cursed. She ran faster, racing back the way she'd come. If he wanted to go back, he'd have to do it on his own. No one would keep her from getting Bryoni and Kent out with her.

She skidded to a stop at the bottom of the hill, steps away from the wolves' den. Breathless, she watched as someone stepped back into the tree line above the ruined city. At that distance, she could have sworn that black hair and muscled build belonged to her father, but she didn't dare call out to him. What if the poachers were nearby and she pointed out his hiding place? She wouldn't be able to live with herself if she put her father in danger.

SHOCK

*P*eridot rushed through the opening in the stone and paused inside, working for breath. Footsteps pounded on the dirt outside, but the wolves didn't react, so Peridot didn't worry. Simran loomed in the doorway a moment before he stepped into the cool darkness beside her.

"I thought you were going back?" Peridot's voice was as cold as the stone surrounding them.

"Alone? I'd never make it." He panted, pressing his palms to his knees to catch his breath. "I don't know my way around here, and I don't have the powers you and your friends have." Peridot didn't answer, so he continued. "Besides, you have all the weapons. What all did you find back there, anyway?"

Peridot tucked the bow and quiver further behind her, away from Simran. "We'll talk when my brother gets back."

A wolf nearby growled at the venom in her tone, so she drew a deep breath tried again, softening her voice.

She jabbed a finger at his chest. "Look, I don't know you. And after what you tried back there, I don't trust you. I'm not telling you anything without the others here to back me up."

"That's fair. I wasn't trying to abandon them, I swear." Simran leaned against the wall, and Peridot watched his movements with interest. He wasn't using his left arm at all, and he twisted awkwardly to avoid touching it to the wall.

"I was just…look, I almost died back there." He gestured to the opening with his right arm. "Maybe getting more help would be the best thing for all of us."

Her eyes narrowed, and Peridot grabbed his arm. "What's wrong with your shoulder? Did I miss something?" She moved the arm through the most basic range of motion. He winced as she raised it over his head. "I did, didn't I? Here, come sit down."

"You don't have to—" He started to argue but cut off mid-sentence, shook his head, and settled onto the sandy ground beside the cave's mouth.

Peridot breathed in, gathering the mountain's energy, and pressed her hand to Simran's right shoulder. Faint emerald light billowed around her hand, and she muttered the words to focus it.

A gasp, then a moan escaped Simran, and he slumped to the ground under her ministrations. Beneath her palm, something snapped into place, and Simran cried out. The light spread down his arm and into his neck, and he whimpered again.

When the light could find no further outlet, it returned to Peridot and she removed her hand, releasing him.

"That wasn't a new injury." Peridot knelt on the ground beside him, exhausted from the outpouring of energy. "That shoulder's been broken for some time. Why didn't you tell me yesterday? I could have fixed it with everything else."

Simran didn't say anything but shook his head and clutched his freshly-healed shoulder. It would hurt for at least the rest of the day, perhaps longer, depending on how long it had been injured.

"What is this power you wield?" He rasped after a while. "Where does it come from? Why can you heal, but she can do so many other things?"

Peridot laughed nervously. "The power comes from the mountain. We can borrow it, but it returns to the mountain when we're finished. As for the rest, it's all about practice and skill. Bryoni goes to lessons to learn all the little tips and charms that let her make fire and cover our tracks and dig holes and such, but I've learned to heal by practicing on myself and the wolves and other creatures of the forest." she shrugged.

"You don't go to lessons?" He met her eyes with an expression of confusion and curiosity.

She leaned back against the wall. "I normally don't bother with the lessons. My family always says I should, and after all this, I'll probably start going more regularly, but I'd rather spend my time in the clean mountain air over a stuffy old classroom. I do practice whenever I can, though."

A jolt of lightning shot through her at his brilliant smile, and she pressed her lips into a thin line.

"I understand that feeling all too well. My grandfather sent me here because he said I wasn't paying enough attention to my own studies. He thought the mountain air would help." Simran laughed. "So far, it's making me want to go to your lessons. I want to learn to heal as you do."

Heat flushed her cheeks, and Peridot dropped her gaze to the dirt. Simran's warm hand cupped her chin, forcing her face up until her eyes met his.

"If we get out of this alive, can I…" He trailed off and coughed. "May I have permission to court you? I'd very much like to get to know you better."

Peridot's mind rushed back to her parents and their absurd expectation that she'd consider marrying Lord Maksym. Maybe if she had another prospect, they wouldn't be in such a hurry to marry her to an old man.

She smiled despite herself. "Yes, I think I'd like that, too."

He leaned close, his hand still cupping her chin. She couldn't fight the attraction, even though she was still annoyed with him. She watched his approach for a heartbeat, closed her eyes, and tipped her head back.

"Hey! Peri, are you there?" Kent's voice echoed from outside the cave.

Peridot's eyes shot open and she jumped away from Simran's grasp. "Yes, I'm here," she called. She dragged a ragged breath in through clenched teeth and stiffened her spine. She couldn't let Kent see her so flustered. He'd pester her relentlessly until she told him why she had so much color in her cheeks.

"You can come on in. The wolves won't bother you," she called when Kent didn't appear.

Nothing.

Peridot tensed and grabbed her bow. His voice had

sounded so close. Were the poachers using him to draw her out? The possibility set her teeth on edge.

Instead of risking being seen in the main entrance, Peridot ducked past several sleeping wolves and moved around to the side of the broad cavern. The opening there wasn't large enough to allow a sprite to enter or exit the cave, but it was perfectly positioned to see the broad opening in the rock face.

A hundred paces in front of the entrance, Bryoni stood, her hands extended toward the forest. A wall of orange light surrounded her. Peridot watched, transfixed, as an axe flew toward her friend and bounced harmlessly off the light.

"Get inside," Bryoni grunted.

"After you're in," Kent said. "I won't leave you to face them alone." He reached out to grab her arm, but she stepped back and to the side, out of his reach.

"Together, then. We need the field to keep them from seeing where we go. Do you know how to summon your power?"

"I think I can boost yours, but I can't do anything on my own."

"That'll work. Remember: pull the energy up through your feet and into your chest. Then send it out to me."

Kent nodded and set his hands beside hers, adding his power to the wall of light. It flared brighter, blinding in its intensity even beneath the midmorning sun. They backed toward the cave while it grew. When it threatened to burst into white-hot flames, both Bryoni and Kent dropped their hands and ran for the entrance to the cave.

Ducking away from the window, Peridot hurried to

meet her friends. She ran headlong into Simran, her nose smashing into his muscled chest.

"I thought only women here had powers? How did he help?"

"Well…" Peridot backed up and wiped a hand under her nose to check for blood. Her eyes watered against the pain, but her hand came away clean. "Yes and no. The men here have powers, but they don't use them."

"Why not?" Simran screwed up his face in a look of outrage and confusion, and Peridot couldn't suppress a laugh.

"I don't know, exactly. Something about being strong enough without it, and relying on magic is seen as a sign of weakness." She shook her head at Simran's baffled expression. "It doesn't make much sense to me, either. Now, come on. They should be back by now."

Peridot didn't wait for an answer but instead turned to the cave's entrance.

The wall of light stayed in place for several long minutes after Bryoni and Kent ducked into the cavern. Peridot watched until the light started to fade and pulled them deeper into the cave.

"Did you get the bow? Were there enough arrows?" Kent whispered.

Peridot met Kent's eyes over the mass of furry beasts and grinned. "Yes. And something else, too."

She couldn't help turning the grin toward Simran. She leaned the bow against the wall and swung the quiver she'd retrieved from the city around in front of her. She set it carefully on the ground and pulled the arrows out. She leaned them point down beside the bow and stuck her hand back into the quiver. At the bottom, she felt for the small wooden box. The smooth wood burned her hand as if she'd grabbed a burning coal, but she closed her fingers around it and pulled it out into the open. It was about the size of Peridot's palm, square, and just large enough to be mistaken for a tinder box. Its finish was such a dark brown it looked black in the dim cave, but thousands of tiny mother-of-pearl insets formed an intricate image of flowers and trees. A soft blue light filtered through the crack between the lid and the body of the box.

"Is that..." Bryoni trailed off, reaching for the box. "Is it really?"

Peridot beamed. "It is." She handed the small wooden container to her friend.

"Would you care to fill us in?" Kent snapped.

"It's a Prandium box." Bryoni whispered, awestruck, turning it over and over in her hands. "Whatever you put inside turns into something to eat. I've heard of them, but I've never seen one before."

"That's incredible!" Simran's hands hovered over the box, but he didn't try to touch it. "Does it really work?"

Grinning, Peridot pulled the top from the box and set it aside. "It does. Watch." She glanced around for something suitable and found a small twig. She set the stick inside the box, replaced the lid, and waited. The light flared, the heat on her hand grew nearly unbearable. Gently, she set it on the ground and watched until the light faded back to the faint glow it had been in the beginning.

"Well, let's see what it did." She pulled the top off the box with a flourish, revealing a stick of dried meat the same shape as the twig she'd inserted. "Here. Try it." She handed the meat to Simran, whose brown eyes shone with a ravenous hunger.

Without fanfare, he bit into the meat, chewed for a moment, and shoved the whole thing in his mouth.

"Why does he get to go first? I'm starving, too." Kent's playful whine made Peridot smile even wider.

"Get some more sticks, leaves, things like that. It has to be something that was once alive, so rocks won't work," she said when Simran tried to hand her a palm-sized stone.

Kent and Bryoni scrambled to find more objects to put in the box. Peridot dropped to her knees to help them. A warm hand closed over her shoulder, and she looked up into Simran's soft brown eyes. A spark shot between them, and Peridot froze in place, one hand resting on the soft sand.

"Will this work?" Kent asked.

Peridot dragged her gaze from Simran's and glanced at the leaves in her brother's hand.

"Yes, that'll do nicely." She took the leaves and placed them in the box. Again, the light flared. When she reopened the box, the leaves had turned to thin slices of meat and berries.

They continued searching and transforming objects to food until they'd each had their fill.

Peridot lifted the box, set it carefully back into the quiver, and arranged the arrows so the points sat safely around it. She slung the quiver over her shoulder and handed the other one to Kent, then chose her favorite of the two bows and gave the other to her brother.

"Now two of us are armed." She grinned to hide the fear welling up in her abdomen. "Besides your sword, Bry.

I don't want to let them get close enough for you to use that. What's next?"

"I think we should head home," Bryoni started.

Simran nodded vigorously and opened his mouth, but Bryoni cut him off. "And tell my father and your father about all of this. We can get a group together to face the poachers and chase them out of our forest."

"Our father's already out here." Kent pointed to the cave's entrance. "I saw him at least three times while we were out there but never got close enough for him to see us. I didn't dare yell for him, not with the poachers so close."

"I saw him, too." Peridot followed her brother's gaze to the brilliant green foliage beyond the stone walls. "What if the poachers get him? He's not even trying to keep hidden."

"We should find him and bring him back with us," Bryoni said, "but I don't think we should try to take on those men by ourselves."

"I don't know. Your father should be able to manage for a little while." Simran straightened his shirt and squared his shoulders. "I think we should get the rest of the villagers and come back for him."

Bryoni narrowed her eyes and examined Simran, and Peridot realized again how little she knew about the man she'd agreed to court. She inspected him from the top of his apple-green hair, down his pointed features––though she avoided meeting his eyes––to his tattered red linen shirt and down to his cotton trousers. She even examined the shoes on his feet, which were of fine leather and fastened with a row of buckles. They were much fancier than any Peridot had seen in their small village.

"Do I pass your inspection?" Simran laughed, but it sounded off. He ducked his head as if to meet her gaze, but she turned away.

Before she could think of anything to say, Kent asked the first question that rang through Peridot's mind. "You're not from here. How did you end up in our forest?"

"Does it matter? Really." Bryoni huffed and stepped up beside Simran. "The poachers nearly beat him to death and kept him tied up. Clearly, he's not on their side. Let's get out of here, then we'll figure everything out."

Kent frowned, Simran looked relieved, and Peridot fought a wave of disappointment. She'd hoped she was about to learn something about the mysterious stranger.

"I'll cover us with a barrier like the one that got us inside," Bryoni offered. "That should get us most of the way up the hill. You're both armed now, so you can cover our backs until we're in the forest, right?"

Peridot nodded. "Where are we headed? Home? Back to the camp? We can't just follow my father around all day, but I don't like the thought of leaving him here."

"He's spent almost as much time in the forest as you lately, so I'll bet he'll be all right even without our help." Kent said. Peridot scowled, and Kent held out his hands in a sign of surrender. "All right. I didn't think you'd go for that. Let's just get into the forest and see if we can spot him." Kent sighed, fatigue heavy in his voice even though it was still only midmorning. "Maybe he'll be close by, and we can get him and go home."

They all agreed on that plan, and Bryoni moved to the cave's entrance.

The escape went exactly as they'd planned. They made

it to the top of the hill and into the forest without any signs of the poachers––or Peridot's father.

"Now what?" Peridot whispered.

"Let's check the camp. We need to make sure they didn't catch him." Kent sounded as if that was the absolute last thing he wanted to do. "You know the forest better than anyone else. You lead."

Before she headed toward the camp, Peridot made a circle of the area where she'd seen her father an hour earlier, searching for footprints or some other sign that she'd actually seen what she thought she had. In the dirt several paces from where she stood, a large indentation caught Peridot's attention. She stepped up to it, followed the direction it pointed, and froze. Three sets of tracks converged there. One set was smaller, the appropriate size to belong to Peridot's father. The other two sets were nearly twice the size of the first.

The tracks facing each other were deeper than elsewhere, so Peridot guessed her father had confronted the others. Nearby, the tracks shifted. The larger prints repositioned themselves behind the smaller ones and deepened there. Why had they stopped? They led off through the forest with the two sets of larger prints staying just behind the smaller set.

"Oh, that doesn't look good," Bryoni whispered. "Do you think he'll be able to get away?"

Peridot grimaced. "Let's hope so."

Shaken, Peridot crept through the forest, not making a sound. As they had the day before, they stayed off the game trails and hunters' paths but kept the other prints in sight.

Peridot led the way, pausing every few steps to listen

to the forest. Overhead, dragons wheeled and called, adding their voices to the forest's song. When their path crossed the stream, the friends stopped to drink. Peridot filled her water canister and sated her thirst before she stood and faced the others.

"We're almost to the camp. Does anyone have any idea what to do when we get there? What do we do if they have my father? What if they're not there at all?"

Kent shook his head and tipped his head back to watch the dragons. "I don't know. Let's see what we find when we get there."

After she'd waited a moment for anyone else to speak, Peridot hopped over the stream and continued through the forest. They descended and climbed hill after hill, working their way ever closer to the poachers' camp but circling around so they stayed between the camp and the trail leading home. Peridot fought the urge to hold her breath.

Voices carried on the wind, and Peridot froze, listening. They were too far away to distinguish words, but the deep timbre distinguished them as men's voices.

Peridot met Kent's wide, terrified eyes and tried to convey a confidence she didn't feel. If the poachers had captured her father, how would she get him free? They weren't likely to fall for the same tricks that had worked the day before.

Without making a sound, she lowered herself beneath the level of the brush and crawled forward. When she reached the edge of the clearing, she eased the bushes to the sides to make an opening wide enough to see and peered into the camp. Her heart caught in her throat, and she nearly choked.

Her father sat on a downed log in the center of the camp. The poachers sat beside him, chatting and laughing. He wasn't bound or injured like Kent and Simran had been the day before. In fact, he laughed at something one of the poachers had said. While Peridot watched, one of the women came out of the tent and handed him a tankard of liquid, which he accepted with a broad smile.

Peridot eased herself back, away from the clearing. Horror and confusion warred in her mind. She concentrated hard, working to hear the men's conversation from her hiding place.

I've misunderstood something, somehow. There's no way...

"Don't much care about the rest, really just need some dragon eggs," one man said.

"I'd put that thought out of your mind." Peridot recognized her father's voice, and her stomach dropped. "Those dragons aren't tame. Even if you get an egg and somehow manage to hatch it, it won't be a pet."

"The stories from the giants' cities all show humans and sprites riding dragons, so there must be a way."

"Haven't you figured it out yet?" Her father sounded exasperated. "The giants made up stories just for entertainment. They're not real. They were never real."

"Well, I don't believe that. Why would they have thousands of stories and paintings that had no basis in truth?"

"Look, I don't understand it, either, but it is what it is. Those stories aren't true. Our people have lived in the shadow of those mountains for hundreds of years, and none have ever managed to ride the dragons."

Behind her, someone stumbled. Gravel crunched underfoot. A twig snapped.

"What was that?" her father's voice sounded alarmed.

"It's probably nothing. The deer have been active here lately." The man her father had been talking to laughed and took a loud slurp of his drink.

"We should make sure," a woman's voice said. "What if the ones that got away come back?"

"Kill them. We can't have them exposing us to everyone in the village." The ruthless cold in her father's voice chilled Peridot to her core.

"What a waste that would be." It was the woman again. "They're worth a fortune in the market back home. Did you see that weakling running this morning? How'd he get so strong all of a sudden?"

Kent retched, the noise echoing through the clearing and bouncing off the trees. A hollow pit opened in Peridot's stomach. They couldn't disguise that as an animal noise.

WOLVES

*P*eridot whispered her instructions over her shoulder. "Run! Head back to the city. We can hide in the caves!" She took off through the trees, hoping the others followed.

While she ran, Peridot pulled out her bow and knocked an arrow. The twang of a bowstring behind her told her Kent had done the same. Peridot whispered a word of thanks to the mountain spirits her father had never bothered to learn either archery or his powers since he'd worked for Lord Maksym's estate at such a young age.

Bryoni caught up to her, stopped, and turned on the trail. Peridot barely avoided a collision and turned an astonished glare on her friend. At least until Bryoni raised her hands and something exploded in the forest behind them.

"That won't stop them for long. Let's go!" Bryoni tugged on Peridot's sleeve, but she didn't need any convincing.

Peridot spun and raced through the forest beside her best friend with Kent's breathing loud in her ear. She slowed her steps for a heartbeat and listened for Simran. His breath mingled with Kent's, so she picked up her pace once more. She paid no heed to the sticks and rocks shifting and snapping under her feet. She'd worry about being quiet later. For now, she had to get as far ahead of the poachers as she could.

As she ran, her father's icy voice echoed in her mind. *"Kill them."* Her stomach tied itself in knots, but her legs moved faster than she'd thought possible.

They reached the edge of the forest where it looked out on the wolves' cave, but Peridot skidded to a halt. There, between them and the cave, one of the men and one of the women from the poachers' camp paced in front of the entrance.

"How'd they beat us here?" Bryoni's breathless question echoed Peridot's stunned thoughts. Footsteps pounded in the forest behind them.

"They must not have been at the camp." Kent panted. "They were here, waiting for us to come back. Let's keep going. Where's the next best place, Peri?"

Peridot shook her head and took off into the forest at a breakneck pace. She didn't know where to go. A woman's scream pierced the air, mingling with the snarling of wolves and a man's shout of pain. Peridot's feet slowed of their own accord, and she stepped to the edge of the wood. The man and woman were surrounded by the wolves who snapped and snarled at the strangers in their midst. At the man's feet, the remains of the yearling bear the wolves had taken down that morning glistened in the afternoon sun.

"They got too close to the food," Peridot breathed. Something crashed in the forest above them, reminding Peridot of the chase and its stakes. She turned back to the forest and raced up the steep mountainside.

"Dot! This way!" Bryoni pointed to the right, toward a sheer cliff face with a waterfall tumbling over the side. "We can get away!"

Peridot stared, confused, as her friends sprinted toward the impossible slope. She trailed behind, her heart in her throat as she considered their predicament. How would they get up the mountain, trapped between the cliff face and the approaching poachers as they were?

"Over here!" Bryoni called. Peridot turned her eyes away from the cliff and spotted her friends hurrying into a crevice in the rock.

Once she'd turned the corner and huddled into the cramped space with the others, Peridot turned questioning eyes on Bryoni. "What are you doing? The path is over there! We're trapped!"

"No, we're not, but they will be."

Peridot started to question further, but Bryoni raised her hands and murmured something Peridot couldn't hear. The ground beneath her shifted and moved. It raised several feet in the air, hovering above the forest floor as the poachers and Peridot's father ran into view. Peridot struggled to stay upright and grabbed onto Kent so they could help to balance each other. Simran grabbed Kent's other arm, but Bryoni stood as steady as if she were on solid ground.

A wave of dizzy nausea rolled over Peridot, but she choked it back and kept her eyes focused on her friend.

Bryoni moved her hands as if encouraging a child to stand and whispered, "Up, up, up."

Below, her father shouted a curse. "Go around! This way!" He led the others around the corner and toward the path Peridot had planned to use.

"Can't you—" The woman began

"No, I can't! let's go!" Her father's voice faded as he ran toward the trail.

"They're getting away." The man from the clearing watched, transfixed, as Bryoni raised them up the sheer cliff.

A few heartbeats later, the circle of stony earth stopped level with the top of the cliff. Bryoni stayed perfectly still, holding the dirt steady while Peridot, Kent, and Simran stepped onto the mountainside. When they were all on solid ground, Bryoni leapt off the levitating patch of earth and onto the cliff beside her friends. The instant her foot left the dirt, it crashed to the ground below and scattered, forming a small crater in the ground and sending a cloud of grass and dirt into the air.

They didn't stay to watch the dust settle. Peridot scanned the mountainside, trying to get her bearings and figure out their best escape route. The village wasn't an option from there, since they'd have to get back down the mountain and the poachers were on the only safe route down. Unless…

"Bryoni," Peridot blurted. "What else can you do? Can you fly us off the mountain and down into the plains so we can get help?" She pointed at the flat ground between their location and the village off in the distance.

"No. I, um, no. I wasn't even sure I could lift us up this

far. I'm nowhere near strong enough to carry us anywhere."

"Where do we go from here?" Kent asked, scanning the forest in front of them.

"I...I'm not sure. I mean, I know where I set the traps from here, but I don't know where we could hide. That wind's getting wild, and it won't be long before we won't be able to walk through the forest at all."

Simran stalked toward the closest game trail. "What does the wind have to do with anything? We need to get off this mountain and get help."

"Look, I know you're new here and all." Kent grabbed Simran's arm and yanked him back. "but you should probably listen when my sister tells you things may get dangerous. No one knows this mountain like she does. Peridot, lead the way."

"I...all right." Uncertain, Peridot set off in the direction Simran had been heading. There were caves up higher, but the dragons claimed them. Maybe she could find an unoccupied cave where they could wait out the coming storm. She didn't have any other ideas. She glanced at the sky and hurried into the woods.

They hadn't gone far before dark clouds gathered over the mountain, and the wind whipped the treetops back and forth. "We can't run any more. We'll have to move slower." Peridot stared up at the treetops and wished they could retreat to lower ground.

"Why on earth not? If we walk, they'll catch us." Simran snapped.

Another gust of wind pulled the tops of the trees until they nearly bent in two. At the peak of the gust, the ground beneath their feet lifted in the air. It settled back to its normal position when the wind eased.

Peridot waited until the ground stayed still for a moment before she stepped further into the forest. "That will swallow a sprite whole if you're not careful. Let's go. Stay close to the tree trunks."

"Um, Peri?" Terror lent a tremor to her brother's voice that she hadn't heard before.

"What?" She couldn't really focus on Kent's words because her attention was on the treetops. When the trees stood straight, she dashed forward. When they bent sideways, she stopped and held onto the tree trunks until they set the earth right again.

"What's happening? Why is the ground moving?" Fear filled Kent's voice, which drew her attention down to his face. All the color had drained from it, and he looked pale and deathly in the dim light.

"It's nothing. Well, not nothing. Look up." She waited for the next wind gust. "See how the trees are bending with the wind?"

He stared upwards but clung to the nearest tree trunk. After a moment, he nodded.

"The trees' roots are all tangled together, so they hold each other up when the wind would blow them down. What's happening is that the roots are lifting up with the strong gusts and settling down when the wind eases."

"Oh. That makes sense, I guess." His face relaxed a bit, and Peridot raised her eyes back to the canopy.

"This is absurd. We're wasting time standing here. Let's go." When the ground settled after the next gust, Simran sprinted forward, passing Peridot and the others and racing into the darkening heart of the forest.

The wind whipped through the trees, the ground lifted, and Simran fell into a hole left by the moving roots.

"Simran!" Peridot hurried to him, staying close to the tree trunks and trying to find stable footing. The ground swayed under her feet, but she kept moving, leaping from tree trunk to tree trunk and clinging to low branches for support.

It felt like a year passed before she got to him. She glanced over him, searching for injuries, and winced. His right leg was twisted at an awkward angle, and his foot was pinned beneath the dirt and tangled in the spiderweb of roots.

"I told you to listen to her!" Kent shouted. "Now look at you! We should just leave you here for them to find. What were you thinking?"

"Why? She can just heal me, right?" Simran gestured wildly toward Peridot. "It's not a big deal!"

Peridot, Kent, and Bryoni stared at him as if he'd lost his mind. Peridot caught herself gaping and snapped her mouth shut.

"I mean…It's not, is it?" The first hint of concern crept onto Simran's face.

"I'm not good at controlling the healing power unless I'm safe," Peridot muttered through gritted teeth. "And you don't want to see what happens if I lose control of it. We'll have to splint that for now and find someplace to hide."

"You've slowed us down…*again.*" Kent spat the words even as he bent to pick up a couple of straight branches. He snapped off the smaller twigs and leaves and ripped several strips off the bottom of his shirt. "This was my favorite," he grumbled and tied the branches to the sides of Simran's leg.

When the splint was secure, Kent wrapped an arm around Simran's chest and lifted the injured man off the forest floor.

"And now you're bleeding, which will make us more interesting to the wildcats and scavengers—and maybe the dragons. Are you always this reckless?" Kent didn't give him a chance to answer before he staggered forward, taking Simran's weight so the injured man could hop along beside him.

The group moved slower than they had before, but they made steady progress toward the caves Peridot had seen below the timber line. As they moved, the animals in the underbrush fell silent and the small hairs on Peridot's neck stood up. She couldn't quite shake the feeling she was being watched, though she didn't see anyone behind or in front of their group. Soon, even the birds in the trees stopped chirping, and the eerie silence made Peridot's stomach do flips. Only the sound of the wind whistling through the trees filled the air around them, and when they spoke, Peridot's group kept their voices to a whisper.

Peridot stopped frequently to look behind and around them, searching endlessly for the source of the forest's unease.

Nothing.

Peridot's heart hammered in her chest, and her breath came in shallow gasps, partly from the exertion of moving through the forest with the ground moving every few steps, and partly from the terror of not knowing what or who stalked them in the trees.

When a little old man appeared on the path in front of her, Peridot let out an involuntary shriek. She immediately clapped her hand over her mouth, fearful that she'd alerted the poachers to her location. The sprite on the path was a slender, pallid man with tufts of white hair sticking out of his head at odd angles. He wore an odd assortment of furs, all sewn together into something resembling breeches and a tunic. A belt at his waist held several knives and a few little bottles that caught the light and shimmered. He watched Peridot in silence, a concerned expression written across his weathered features.

"Who...Who are you?" Peridot managed to stammer. "Are you the o— the man the villagers talk about? The one who moved up to the mountain and never came back? They say you're dead."

The man smiled but didn't answer. Instead, he pointed to the left. "If you want to get out of this wind, come with me."

He strode away through the forest at a reckless pace, but Kent and Simran couldn't keep up. Peridot hung back to keep from leaving her brother behind, though she would have gladly left Simran after his stupid sprint through the forest.

The little man doubled back to see where they were and eyed Simran with a dismissive gaze. He met Peridot's eyes, apparently deciding she was in charge since she'd been the one to speak to him before. "You are aware you're being followed?"

"Yes, but I wasn't sure they were still behind us or if they'd turned back, you know, because of the wind and all." Peridot silently cursed her nervous chatter but stepped closer to the man. "You said you know some-where safe where we can hide?"

"I said I know a place where you can get out of the wind. You can heal that one there." He jerked his head toward Simran. "The mountain loves you, though she cares not for the others with you. I will help you, at her request. They are not my concern."

Peridot hesitated but decided to try again. "If I may ask, sir, what can I call you?"

He said nothing. Instead, he disappeared between the trees and re-materialized several paces in front of her.

She hovered near Kent and Simran, though Bryoni moved faster to keep the stranger in her sight. As long as Peridot could see Bryoni, she stayed as relaxed as she could be in her current situation. At least the birds and squirrels had given up their vows of silence, and the crickets had resumed their calls.

"Ouch! Be careful!" Simran snapped behind her. "That's really sore."

Kent gave him a little shove forward. "You wouldn't be hurt if you had listened to Peridot and stayed with the rest of us. Keep quiet. We need to try to keep up and *not* announce to the poachers where we are."

Peridot shot Simran a withering look and considered what she could say to add to her brother's admonition, but couldn't think of anything.

Something growled from behind the bushes, and all the color leeched out of Simran's face. Bryoni turned back at the sound and raised her hands. A soft yellow light surrounded them. Peridot hoped it was some sort of force field that would either hide them from the forest creatures or protect them from attack, though she didn't know which, if either, it was.

The growl was enough to silence Simran, however, and he hopped faster than ever at Kent's side. Together they moved through the forest almost as fast as Peridot, and she only had to stop once every fifty paces to let them keep her in view.

Cold drops of rain fell through the canopy, pelting Peridot's head and shoulders and stinging like icicles on the bare skin of her face. She wished she'd brought her hooded cloak along, but she hadn't expected to spend so much time in the wilderness, and she hadn't thought she'd be out in the rain. The morning sky had been crystal clear when they'd left her home the day before.

The little man vanished somewhere in the forest and Bryoni spun in a slow circle, searching for him. Peridot's confidence wavered and died. Should she continue in the same direction? Or follow one of the game trails in the hope it would lead to shelter? Before she had to choose one or the other, he reappeared beside her. Startled, Peridot gasped.

"You spend many hours on this mountain. She cares for you as you care for her creatures. Why are you so easily frightened?"

Peridot didn't have an answer to that. She normally wasn't easy to scare, but the past two days had been anything but normal.

The old man cocked his head and glanced behind her. "Is it the strange sprites following you? Do they frighten you?"

"Yes," Peridot answered truthfully. "They do. They

want to either kill me or sell me as a slave. I don't think it much matters which to them."

The man's green eyes flashed. "They will accomplish neither. Come. The rain is here." He spoke in low, throaty tones that made his words difficult to distinguish, but Peridot didn't have time to puzzle it out before he took off ahead of her.

He led them to a cave beneath a massive tree, its roots pulling and trying to hide the small opening. "You may hide here. Do not venture deeper into the cave. Stay close to its mouth, and you will be safe. The mountain will keep your secret."

The man glared at Simran and stalked off through the forest. Peridot watched him go, but the rain increased and fell in blinding sheets, so she ducked into the hole. The cave was tall enough to stand up in, which surprised her, but it was a steep drop down from the ground above. The opening almost reached her chest.

"Kent," she called. "Come down here and help me so we can get Simran in."

He did as she asked, and Bryoni hopped in after him. Together, the three of them lowered Simran to the ground inside the cave and helped him back far enough from the opening that they wouldn't get wet.

"It's a wonder you're not dead yet." Peridot knelt beside Simran and drew a breath. She focused on the mountain's energy and let it fill her chest. When she could hold no more, she pressed a hand to his deformed leg. He gasped in pain, but otherwise kept quiet. Soft emerald light filled the cave as Peridot focused on healing the leg. Both bones in the lower leg had snapped, and they ground against each other and popped back into their proper place.

Kent groaned and gagged.

"Hush. You'll give us away." Peridot kept her eyes on her work, though there wasn't much left to do. The veins and tendons reknit themselves beneath her touch, and warmth flooded into the swollen ankle.

A soft grunt escaped Simran at the return of circulation to his foot, but he kept it quiet.

"I know it smarts. It'll hurt for tonight and should be worlds better by morning." Peridot glanced out the cave's opening. "It doesn't look like we're getting out of here tonight. We should find some sticks and leaves and things to convert to food. I don't have much water left, so I guess we should be thankful for the rain."

As if the forest itself had heard her, a rivulet of rainwater drizzled in through the cave's mouth and ran toward the perimeter, where it vanished through a palm-sized hole in the floor and echoed softly off the stone underneath. Peridot yanked her pack off her back, grabbed her water canister, and held it beneath the stream until the water reached its top. She re-corked the bottle and ducked closer. She drank from the cold, fresh stream until her thirst abated. When she'd finished, Kent and Bryoni took turns drinking, and Peridot handed Simran the canister so he could rehydrate. She refilled it when he'd finished, and the three uninjured sprites scanned the cave's floor for sticks and leaves that would fit into Peridot's box.

While they ate, the rain slowed, and the orange light of sunset filtered into the cave. The wind howled and whistled through the trees and caverns, but Peridot thanked the mountain they wouldn't end up completely soaked from sleeping on the wet ground.

They each ate their fill of the dried meat, berries, and nuts the box produced, and Peridot leaned back against the cave's cold wall. Her father's face popped into her mind, unbidden. He had told the poachers to kill them. How could he wish his own son and daughter dead? What was he tangled up in that their deaths seemed preferable to exposure? He'd been distracted and irritable for more than a year but had blamed it on his age and concern for his children. Could he have done something to try to secure a more lucrative retirement? Her mind circled round and round but produced no answers.

"What do we do when we get home?" Kent asked, his voice soft and sad. "We can't go to Mother. Clearly, Father's involved in all this somehow. We don't know what she knows or if she's involved, too. Who can we trust?"

Fear and grief shone in Bryoni's soft brown eyes. "We can go to my father. I know he's trustworthy. He's been talking about all the weird puncture wounds he's found on the sheep lately. It sounds like what you found on the wolves the other day."

"What about Lord Maksym? Should we go to him?" Kent frowned. "I know you don't like him much, Peri, but he is the one in charge of the village."

"No." Simran's sharp retort caught Peridot off guard. She waited, but he didn't elaborate.

"Why not? Kent's right. He's the one in command of the village."

"But didn't you say your father works for the local lord? What if he's working with the poachers on his boss's orders?"

Peridot considered that. It was a possibility, and it

made more sense than her father doing something like this on his own. She wished she had someone she could trust, someone older and wiser who could tell her what to do. Exhaustion and worry warred in her mind, but the fatigue won out. She leaned her head back against the cave's wall and slept.

$\sim$

"She doesn't have to know. What's the worst that could happen?" Whispered voices pulled Peridot out of her slumber.

"You heard the old man. The mountain doesn't care if we die. It'll protect her. I think if anyone's going to go exploring in this cave, it should be Peridot." That was Kent's voice.

"I don't know. I don't think he would have said anything if there wasn't danger involved in traveling deeper into the cave. He doesn't seem like the kind of sprite that makes things up for fun."

"Don't be absurd. We've been here all night and haven't even seen so much as a beetle. There's nothing here."

Kent scoffed. "To be honest, I don't have any faith in your judgment after the way you acted yesterday."

Peridot opened her eyes at the venom in her brother's voice. Soft gray light streamed through the cave's mouth. She stretched her arms and legs with the slightest movements she could manage but didn't sit up. She wanted to hear what her friends would decide to do without her input.

"Well, if she hadn't been creeping through the woods

at a snail's pace, I wouldn't have tried to go ahead. If we'd stayed at the pace she set, they would have caught us for sure." Simran sounded so sure of himself, Peridot fought back a bitter laugh.

"You do realize we went much slower after you hurt yourself than we did before, right?" Bryoni's voice wasn't much friendlier than Kent's.

Perhaps she'd been too hasty in agreeing to court this man yesterday, Peridot mused. She didn't know anything about him, and he'd shown he wasn't great at navigating her beloved mountain. Peridot ran through all Simran's words and actions in the brief time she'd known him, searching her memory for some sign of courage or wit or cunning that could redeem him after his behavior on the mountainside. She couldn't think of any. Sure, there was physical attraction, that zing whenever his hand brushed her arm or her hand touched him to heal his wounds, but was that enough? She wasn't sure. She'd watch him closely until they made it back to the village. That way she could either accept his advances with confidence or reject them with equal certainty.

"Look, I'm going in. You can stay here like obedient little children if that makes you happy, but I want to know what's down in this cave."

Peridot sat up. "I wouldn't do that. These caves are occupied most of the time. I can only guess at what powers that sprite used to give us shelter for the night, but I promise he won't save you if you endanger yourself here."

Simran pushed himself to his feet, testing out his newly-healed leg. Apparently satisfied that it would hold him, he strolled toward the back of the cavern.

"I'm going to explore. I've never seen caves like this before, and I'm not going to miss my chance to see what kind of animals live in these."

"I can tell you what you're likely to find, if it would change your mind," Peridot offered, fighting back a little grin. "But I won't go in with you. Not when I've received such a warning not to."

"You can't change my mind. I'm going. If you're not interested, that's fine. Wait here, and I'll be back in a while." He turned his back to Peridot and the others.

"If you go, you'll die." Peridot whispered. "I can't save you from the creatures that live inside the mountain."

Simran didn't answer. Instead, he pushed himself away from the cave's stone wall and stalked away into the blackness.

"Well, does anyone want to go along?" Kent didn't bother to whisper. Bryoni and Peridot both shook their heads. "We should eat something. Are there any more sticks in here?"

They searched for anything they might have missed the night before, and each had a handful of food to chew on before the morning light grew any brighter.

A piercing scream echoed through the cave, originating somewhere deep in the mountain.

"That didn't last long." Kent didn't sound concerned at all, but Peridot's heart slammed against her ribs.

"We have to get out." Peridot whispered. "He's awakened the dragons."

Kent went pale. Bryoni cried out in terror. All three ran for the cave's entrance and scrambled out into the blinding morning sun.

"Get behind a big tree and crouch down!" Peridot

yelled even as she followed her own advice. "Make yourself as small and nonthreatening as you can."

"Shouldn't we run?" Kent crouched behind a tree near Peridot's and lost his breakfast onto the still-damp ground.

Peridot shook her head. "We can't outrun them. They can fly, remember? Besides, running makes you look like food."

"Oh." Kent sounded ill.

He retched again, and Peridot fought the urge to roll her eyes. He'd had a hard few days—even harder than hers since he'd been captured before they'd broken him free and gone on the run.

Peridot turned her attention to the rumbling and screeching coming from the cave. Part of her hoped to see Simran come running out, but she knew that wasn't likely. He'd disturbed a clutch of dragons in their lair. They weren't known for letting intruders run free.

As if to confirm her suspicions, the first dragon to fly out of the opening beneath the tree had blood dripping from the talons on his front feet.

"Don't move." Peridot barely even dared to move her lips to utter the warning.

The dragons flew in widening circles around and over the tree above the cave, searching for any more intruders. The screams and growls they uttered struck terror in Peridot's bones, but she stayed frozen behind her tree. She couldn't see Kent or Bryoni without turning her head, and the slightest move could draw the dragons' attention, so she stayed as still as the toppled stone statues in the square and prayed to the mountain that her brother and her best friend could fight the fear response and keep themselves from running.

She stayed like that for an eternity while more and more dragons exited the cave. After a while, they settled down and the angry cries quieted into normal calls.

An odd, misplaced sound grabbed her attention and she poked her head around the tree, ready to retreat once more if the noise proved to be dangerous. Thump and slide, thump and slide, the sound repeated again and again. Peridot blinked several times, unwilling to believe her traitorous eyes. Simran was there. Bleeding, limping, crawling, and sometimes dragging himself forward. His right arm had been ripped off below the elbow and left a trail of brilliant scarlet in the dirt behind him. Punctures and deep lacerations covered his legs, and a cut along his neck bled ominously, but he was alive. Peridot gaped and dashed from her hiding spot to drag him to safety. Somewhere nearby, Kent retched.

Peridot fought a wave of nauseated horror and propped Simran against the nearest tree. "What were you thinking?" She pressed one hand to the spurting stump of his arm and the other to the gash on his neck. "I can't heal this all the way right now. There isn't time. I'll have to close it up and try to fix it later."

He nodded weakly but didn't attempt to speak. Sweat beaded across Peridot's forehead and upper lip. She'd never been great at controlling her powers and was even worse at using them while in danger, but if she didn't do something, he'd bleed to death. Based on the pallor in his lips and cheeks, she guessed he had only a minute or two left if she didn't stop the bleeding. She closed her eyes and tried to block out the dragons' calls, focusing all her energy on the barely-alive man in front of her. She breathed in, pulling the power in through her feet. She muttered the words to make the healing charm work, and a faint green light grew around them.

The bleeding from his arm and neck stopped first. When those wounds had scabbed over, she shifted her attention to his legs. She stopped the bleeding there and focused with all her might on his inner force, restoring as much of his blood supply as she could before she collapsed, exhausted, on the ground in front of him.

Overhead, the dragons circled and called out to each other. Peridot opened her eyes and watched them swoop and dive. One came up with a deer dangling from its front claws. It dove toward the cave with its catch. Peridot rolled closer to the tree and sat up, bracing her back against the rough trunk. She pulled Simran up beside her and motioned for him to stay quiet. She fretted about his pallor and considered trying again to replenish his blood, but she didn't have much faith in her ability to heal him and not leave herself completely drained. She'd have to get him somewhere safe first.

They waited in silence until most of the dragons had followed the deer into the cave. When it was safe, or as safe as it could be with the poachers in the forest, Peridot stood and motioned the others over.

"Is this why they called you 'the weakling'?" Kent blurted the words as soon as he stepped close enough to be heard without shouting. "Because you're constantly doing stupid things and getting yourself hurt? Worse yet, endangering everyone you're with?"

"I'm not—"

Peridot cut him off. "We'll have time to discuss this all

later. Right now, we need to get moving." She raised her eyes to the few dragons still gliding through the air. "You'd better believe the poachers saw those dragons circling and are on their way to investigate. They want an egg, remember?"

Bryoni raised her hands as if to use her powers, scanned the immediate area, and dropped her arms.

"Do you know where we are?" Kent looked to Peridot. "Or how to get us home?"

RUINS

Peridot turned in a slow circle, looking for familiar landmarks. "I…I think so, but I've never seen that cave before, so I'll have to walk a bit to make sure." She gave Simran a hard look. "Can you walk? Or are we carrying you again today?"

She frowned, realizing that when she'd healed him this time, she'd felt none of the electric attraction she'd experienced before. Maybe all the trouble he'd caused had killed any spark that may have existed. That, or seeing him bleeding to death on the dirt was enough to silence her baser instincts. She didn't know which it was or if both factors had played into the change.

"I think I can walk." Simran refused to meet her eyes, and instead kept his head down. "Thank you for saving me—again. You would have been right to leave me to bleed to death."

Peridot pressed her lips into a line. "I couldn't do that. Let's go." She set off at a slow pace. She needed to figure out where she was, and she worried about pushing

Simran too hard. They'd gone about fifty paces when he spoke up.

"I can go faster than this. They'll catch us in no time if we go this slow all day."

A sarcastic retort sprang to Peridot's lips, but she bit it back. She picked up the pace, but still went slower than they had the day before.

The morning had dawned clear and calm, and Peridot inhaled the mountain's freshly-washed scent. Birds chirped overhead, and small animals rustled in the under-brush. If it weren't for the poachers in the forest some-where, Peridot would have enjoyed such a glorious morning.

The hairs on the back of her neck stood on end. She stopped and glanced around, searching for whatever had triggered that response.

Behind her, Kent shouted. "What's this? Oh!"

Peridot spun, but Kent wasn't there. Her breath caught and she rushed back to where he should have been.

"Up here!" His voice carried down from a high branch.

Peridot tipped her head back and stared. Ropes encir-cled both legs and hung him upside down, too high up for her to reach.

"Bryoni, can you get him down somehow? I could try to shoot the ropes, but that fall would be bad."

A soft thud sounded behind them, and Peridot and Bryoni both glanced back to see Simran lying flat on his back.

"What're you doing?" Peridot screeched. "We can't rest here!"

Bryoni grabbed Peridot's arm and pulled. Twenty

paces from where they stood, the poachers stepped out from behind trees.

Peridot cursed softly and grabbed her bow off her back. She raised it into position and snatched a handful of arrows from her quiver. She shot six arrows in seconds, but only three hit their marks. Two sprouted from the chest of the tallest female, and one dug deep into the only man's shoulder.

She reached back for more arrows, but a hand clamped around her wrist and pulled it down, wrenching her shoulder painfully. Peridot dropped to her knees to ease the pressure and spun to free her arm. Without considering her actions, she brought her bow up and jammed it back into her attacker's face. A woman's scream sounded in Peridot's ear, so she dropped the bow and repeated the move. The second time, it sunk deeper into something soft, and Peridot stood and spun to face her attacker. The bow had impaled the woman's left eye and sunk deep into her skull.

Peridot gagged and jerked the bow free. She wiped it over the mossy ground to remove the blood and reached for her arrows. The woman crumpled to the ground.

A blast of energy hit her from the side. Peridot grunted but kept her feet. She followed the blast with her eyes. The man with an arrow in his shoulder stood behind Bryoni with his arms around her upper arms. Bryoni sent wild blasts of energy in every direction to try to free herself.

"Hedrek!" The man grunted when Bryoni hit him in the face with an orange light. "Can't you counter this somehow?"

Peridot froze at her father's name. She stared wide-eyed as the man she'd always turned to for protection and support stepped out of the trees.

"No, Conar, I can't. Men don't use those powers. We're strong enough without resorting to antique magic. Can't you control that girl? She's half your size." Her father spoke lazily, as if discussing the weather or which vegetable he wanted with his supper.

Betrayal and nausea washed over her, and Peridot lowered her left arm, the one holding her bow, for a heartbeat. That was long enough. A woman with long white hair grabbed the bow and wrenched it out of Peridot's hand. She tossed the bow and grabbed Peridot's wrists, holding them together in one massive hand. Her piercing pink eyes met Peridot's. The rage and hatred there made Peridot cringe even more than the knife she pointed at Peridot's throat.

"You killed my husband," the woman spat. "You will pay."

"Easy, Leigham. We need 'em alive." A male voice said from behind Peridot.

"We really don't. That one's been more trouble than she's worth for years now."

Peridot glared at her father, who stepped into her line of sight behind the woman called Leigham. Desperate, Peridot breathed in. She ignored the pain of the knife digging into the soft flesh at the base of her throat, focused instead on the wild energy of the mountain's power growing in her chest.

"Stop her!" Someone yelled, but Peridot brought her hands up a few inches, though she couldn't break the woman's grasp.

She focused hard on the woman in front of her. Cold

blue light surged around her hands, up her wrists, and to her elbows.

The woman shouted something Peridot didn't understand and released her hold on Peridot. The knife wobbled and dropped to the ground, and Peridot relaxed, exhaling the rest of the energy. She didn't trust herself to try anything more dangerous with her friends in such close proximity. Even Bryoni was struggling to control the powers in their current situation. Peridot cursed softly and wished she had spent more time practicing. Before Leigham recovered the use of her hands, Peridot reached down and grabbed the knife.

She wielded it awkwardly, holding it out between herself and the woman with her elbows locked straight, but it worked. Leigham backed away, her eyes wide with fear and anger.

Focused as she was on the woman in front of her, Peridot didn't hear the other person approaching until a rope slid over her head and around her upper arms. She clutched the knife and brought it up in front of her, but the man behind her laughed. A broad hand reached around and grabbed her wrist, squeezing until she felt the bones buckle and snap. A wave of pain and nausea weakened her knees, but she drew a breath and kept her feet beneath her. The knife dropped from her limp fingers.

She stood, frozen from pain and shock, while the man bound her arms down. While he worked, she turned her attention inward, honing her focus until she knew nothing but the mountain's energy growing in her chest and the pain in her wrist. The pain grew white-hot in the soft glow, and she caught her breath when the bones snapped back into place. The pain sapped the strength from her legs, and she dropped to her knees but didn't break her focus. The nerves and blood vessels reknit themselves and feeling rushed back into her fingers like a million tiny needles. Her eyes watered and her stomach heaved, but Peridot kept the energy going until her wrist felt completely normal. She exhaled. A dark curtain covered her vision, and for an instant, Peridot thought she was about to faint. Only the musty stench of rotten potatoes relieved her of that impression as the man slid the bag further over her shoulders.

Peridot cursed softly, and the man laughed again. "You're a feisty one, aren't you?" He murmured beside her ear. "I bet that's why your father's so eager to get rid of you. Can't have a girl around that's stronger than her papa."

Out of options and unsure what else to do, Peridot drew as deep a breath as she could muster against the ropes binding her chest. She released it all in a piercing scream. The sound echoed off the high mountain cliffs and bounced between the tall trees. Her efforts earned a sharp blow across the face. Her head jerked to the side from the force of the strike, and blood erupted in her mouth. Her vision swam, but she shook it off in the darkness of the sack.

"We won't be drawing attention to ourselves like that, you hear me?" The man said. His voice was soft, but held a deadly edge she wasn't willing to test.

Peridot drew an uneven breath and swallowed a mouthful of blood. She drew a tiny bit of energy from the mountain and closed the cut in her cheek but left the bruises. If she let the man know she could heal whatever damage he caused, it may well encourage him to hurt her more. She marveled for a moment that she'd gained so much control over the mountain's power in only a couple of days.

The world spun as the man lifted her roughly and tossed her over his shoulder. In that moment, Peridot was glad for the bag over her head, so no one could see her cheeks flush with embarrassment. It was the most humiliating position she'd ever been in, and that included the time her sister had pulled her dress up in the market when they were children.

CAPTIVES

The trip down the mountain to the poachers' camp took an eternity. With her head covered, Peridot caught only tiny glimpses of the ground through the holes in the bag's loose weave. She couldn't tell what time of day it was when they stopped. The man dumped her on the ground. He kept her feet to the side so she couldn't stand, and her backside landed on a sharply pointed rock. Her eyes watered with pain, but again she fought the impulse to heal the bruise.

"I don't care what you do with them from here, and maybe it's best if I don't know," Peridot's father said. "I need to get back to the village before anyone suspects something's amiss. I'll tell them the dragons ate these miscreants. Just don't let them get away, or you'll suffer for it."

"They won't get loose; I'll promise you that," a woman's voice answered. Peridot recognized it as the white-haired woman she'd faced on the mountain.

"Good. I'll see you next week in Eriford, then, and you'll have everything we talked about ready, right?"

"Of course. It's easy from here. Now that we know where the caves go, and we don't have to worry about this lot messing it all up, anyway." The man said, his voice eager.

"I wouldn't be so sure," her father sneered.

The camp went quiet except for the sounds of someone building a fire and an occasional murmured request.

Peridot listened for sounds of her friends, but as hard as she strained, she heard nothing but the wind in the trees. She wished she could get the bag off her head. She spent the next hour or so wiggling the ropes up higher on her torso. When she'd freed her forearms and could bend her elbows, she brought her bound wrists up to her neck. She felt for the end of the rope there, found it, and yanked the loose end to untie the bow.

Except it wasn't a bow. The tug had tightened the rope around her neck so the pressure built in her face. Panic blossomed in her belly. She struggled to get her fingers beneath the rope but couldn't loosen it even with both hands under it. The choking pressure increased with her hands under the rope, so she pulled them out and felt for the knot. Desperate and shaking, she found the uppermost loop on the knot and tugged at it until it came free. That released the knot and the rope fell free, dangling from her shoulders.

Footsteps crunched on the gravel nearby. Peridot dropped her arms back down and sat perfectly still, trying her best to look like a docile captive until the person had moved off.

When she couldn't see anyone nearby through the tiny holes in the bag, she lifted it to her forehead and inhaled deeply. The air in the bag had been hot and stuffy, and the fresh mountain air rushing into her lungs made her giddy with relief. She took a quick inventory of the camp. The two remaining women bustled in and out of the tents, gathering tools to cook their evening meal. The man sat beside the fire, poking it with a stick and occasionally tossing more wood onto the pile.

Kent sat much like her with his back against a tree and a bag over his head. As she watched, he worked the bonds on his hands loose and started working to free his shoulders. Thirty paces to his right, Bryoni sat against a tree, but the charred remains of her ropes sat in a neat pile beside her. She met Peridot's eyes and winked. Peridot searched the parts of the camp within her line of sight but could find no trace of Simran. She pictured him slumped on the ground where he'd fallen on the mountain. Had they left him for dead? He'd been badly wounded but could have survived, at least with her help. He'd be dead before daybreak if they'd left him, though. The wolves, cougars, dragons, and bears would have enjoyed such an easy meal. Her heart sunk at the thought, and she hoped they'd moved him into a tent to keep the smell of his wounds from attracting scavengers.

"Any ideas how we're supposed to get the mineral and watch the slaves? They'll fetch a pretty penny if we can keep 'em, but they're slipp'ry."

The woman Peridot had faced stepped up to the fire and dropped a pot onto the frame over it. She pulled cut mushrooms and vegetables out of her pockets, and Peridot frowned. Had her father been taking them vegetables out of the garden? That would explain all the missing food that they'd blamed on raccoons.

Realization dawned, and Peridot froze in horror. No. He hadn't been taking them food. He'd been letting them into their garden at night. That's why they'd been bold enough to come into the garden the night they'd captured Kent. But that meant they'd been there for at least two weeks, sneaking into their town and stealing their food. The woman straightened and glanced over at Kent.

Peridot dropped the hood back over her face and crossed her wrists in her lap as if still bound.

"You're right, Leigham. I don't trust 'em, neither. I think we should leave 'em tied tight tonight and tomorrow, while we gather as much of the mineral as we can carry, and we'll loosen their binds a bit when we're on the road away from here."

"Good idea," the man agreed. "The less chances we give them to escape, the better. Are we gonna take turns keeping watch on them tonight?"

"Nah. You've seen 'em, same as I have. They're nothin' but scared children. They hunker down before the sun sets to wait out the dark. They won't try to run off at night."

Peridot's pulse picked up. She didn't relish the idea of being out in the forest overnight, but she wasn't about to stay where she was and wait to see who the poachers found to sell her to. She settled back against the tree to wait for the poachers to go to bed but found herself listening to their conversations.

"Do you think Hedrek's got the right idea on the crystals?" One of the women asked. "We've been here for weeks and don't have any powers, and we're right on top o' the caves."

"Nah. It's no different from our families and the power they get from the sea. When we leave the coast, our powers evaporate. The same happens to people from the plains. They leave home, they lose their powers." The man poked at the fire, sending up a river of sparks Peridot could see through the sack. "The crystals make the mountain folk's powers stronger because they're from the mountain, just like seashells and driftwood make us stronger."

"So you think we're wasting our time here?" A woman's voice.

"Nope. We've got these, and those, and the captives we can sell for slaves. That's more than enough to make this a profitable trip. 'Sides, there's enough people willin' to spend a pretty penny on those crystals in the city. We'll sell 'em on the way back home."

"But we've lost so much already," a woman whispered. She added something else Peridot couldn't make out, that might have been a list of names. "Is it worth the loss of life?" She asked louder.

A long silence stretched before anyone spoke. The other woman's voice sounded choked and hoarse when she answered. "The sprites here believe that death just means you return to the earth, where you came from. The mountain sprites rejoin the mountain, no matter where they are when they die. Same for all the others. I think that's a good way to think of it. They're back with the sea, where they belong."

The fire crackled, and oil popped, but no one said anything for a long time after that. Peridot tried to

pretend she couldn't smell the meat and vegetables cooking. She worked to ignore the grumbling and growling in
her belly. They'd already said they didn't plan to give her
any of the food, so there was no sense longing for it. She
watched through the bag as the sky darkened. Her bladder
called for release, but she held it and tried her best to
ignore that, too. She'd be free soon enough and would be
able to tend to all her body's needs–including healing the
aching bruises on her face and backside.

The evening dragged on, and Peridot counted the
owls' hoots and birds' calls to pass the time. The poachers'
conversation about their fallen comrades rang in her ears,
and guilt dug a pit in her gut. She fought off the guilt and
told herself they'd still be alive if they hadn't come here, if
they'd left the forest and the wolves and her brother
alone. She worked to tune out anything else the poachers
said and only vaguely listened for the words 'captives' or
'slaves' so she'd have an idea what they planned for her.
She didn't catch any more instances of those words, and
when the sky fell dark, the poachers retreated to their
tents. Peridot tried to see who went to which tents, but all
she knew for certain was that both women went to the
one in the middle. She had no idea which one the man
chose.

She waited a while after they'd disappeared, giving
them time to fall asleep. Soft snores echoed from close by,
and Peridot decided she'd waited long enough. She closed
her eyes and focused first on healing her injuries. She'd
need all her strength to survive this night. When that was
done, the pain still radiated through her cheek and down
her leg, but strength coursed through her muscles. She
ripped the sack off her head and wiggled her way out of

the remaining rope. Across the camp, Kent did the same, and Bryoni stood and strolled toward the fire.

Peridot pushed herself to her feet and stretched. Her muscles ached and complained after so long in one position. She Stretched once more and turned her attention to the camp. She met Kent and Bryoni by the fire where the pops and sizzles would mask their whispered conversation.

"Does anyone see Simran?" Peridot asked first.

The others shook their heads. A sick feeling spread through her gut.

"Should we look for him?"

"Let's check the tents. Maybe we'll find him, but I think they're hiding something else in that one." Bryoni pointed to the far-left tent. They moved together toward the shelter she'd indicated and paused to listen outside the tent flap.

"I'm here," a raspy whisper called from behind the tent they'd been about to search. "I can't get loose."

Peridot froze for half a heartbeat, recognized Simran's voice, and sprinted around the tent. He lay braced between two spindly trees, tied at his knees and ankles and with a heavy rope around his upper arms. A worn burlap sack covered his head, and she released the knot and removed that first. Kent crept up beside her and worked at the ropes binding Simran's legs while Peridot focused her energy on healing him enough to flee. She kept her body between Simran and the tent to block as much of the light as she could, but she moved quickly and healed only the most critical injuries.

"Can you walk?" She whispered when she'd finished.

He nodded and stretched his arms and legs, though his

eyes lingered on the place where his hand should have been.

"They're hiding something there." Simran pointed to a tent a hundred paces from the camp. "They've gone back and forth all night."

Peridot nodded her understanding and motioned Simran and Kent to stay put. She circled around the tent to find Bryoni.

Together, they made a cursory check of the third tent in the camp.

Bags and chests stacked on and under tables filled the tent's perimeter. The clean smell of dirt and vegetables filled the space. This had to be where they kept their supplies. Peridot fought the urge to grab as much food as she could carry. From the corner of her eye, Peridot spotted something, and she moved quickly toward it. Both of her bows and quivers leaned against the tent's corner. They looked exactly the same as the last time she'd seen them, but she held her breath and stalked over to them. She dug to the bottom of the quiver she'd recovered from the city and breathed a sigh of relief. The box was still there. The older of the bows, the one she'd gotten from her closet after she'd broken her favorite, had a crack near the leather grip, but the other looked to be in perfect condition. The light in her palm died when she reached for the bow. Darkness filled the tent, and she waited for her eyes to adjust. She left the damaged bow where it lay against the tent's canvas wall and took both quivers and the intact bow.

Side by side, she and Bryoni left the tent and moved around into the darkened forest to meet her brother and

Simran. They moved as a group toward the lone tent Simran had pointed out.

Bryoni gestured toward the other tents. "I'll stay out here and keep watch. Kent, you watch that way, and I'll watch this way, all right? " She turned her back to the tent flap and faced out into the camp, scanning left to right and back again for any threat.

Kent nodded, and Simran squared his shoulders and stepped up to the tent.

Peridot loosened the ties that held the tent closed and listened for any sounds within.

Nothing.

Her muscles tensed in preparation for a quick retreat, but she rolled her shoulders and ducked into the dark tent. The faint rustling of canvas told her Simran had followed her through.

"Parvum Lumen," she whispered. A tiny white flame appeared above her right palm, which she held out to her side to light the space.

"Over here." Simran tugged her to the right, but she hesitated.

The room swam as her head spun. The tent contained more horrors than she could have imagined. Heads of owls on wooden posts, skinks and larger lizards suspended in green liquid, the wolf furs, and on a platter at the very back of the space, four dragon eggs stacked carefully in a pyramid. Peridot's eyes clung to the exposed infants, and her heart clenched at the thought of their mother's worry.

"Peri, over here."

Peridot startled at Simran's whisper but turned to see what he'd found. He stood before a heavy black curtain in the tent's back left corner. He'd pulled a bit of the curtain aside, but she couldn't see well enough to tell what it concealed. Curious, and yet filled with dread, Peridot crept over and peered into the tiny opening.

There, huddled in the corner of a small cage, a baby dragon stared back at her.

Peridot gasped and gawked, unsure what to do. "If we take that baby out of here, her mother will be on us in an instant. But if we leave her, the poachers will kill her...or worse, sell her."

Simran agreed softly. Together, they stared into the cage.

"We have to save her," Simran murmured. "We can't leave her to them."

"I know," she whispered. She moved all the arrows to the quiver from the city, leaving the second empty. She strode to the table and placed the dragon eggs carefully in the empty quiver, one atop the next. That done, she handed the bow and the quiver with the arrows to Simran.

"Can you shoot this if you have to?"

He shook his head. "I normally can, but..." he held up his severed arm.

Peridot flushed in embarrassment and thanked the mountain that the darkness concealed it. Obviously, he couldn't shoot with his hand missing. She shook off the shock and pressed the bow into his remaining hand.

"Of course," she murmured. In a stronger voice, she said, "I have a better chance of surviving the dragons, so I'll take the baby. Give that to Kent, so he can cover us from behind, but no matter what happens, don't let him shoot at the dragons."

Simran accepted the weapons with a nod and pulled on the cage door. It swung open soundlessly, and Peridot reached an arm inside. The tiny dragon was barely the size of a wolf pup, but it spat and clawed at her arm until she withdrew to come up with another plan.

Faint green light filled the tent as Peridot healed the cuts from the infant's claws. How could she get the baby out? She certainly couldn't carry the whole cage into the forest. While she considered the problem, she rekindled the tiny light in her palm and examined the outside of the cage. She smiled a bit when she realized the right side of the cage front folded out, which would provide a much larger opening. She located the release and swung the panel on its hinges. The dragon responded by cringing down into the furthest corner of the cage.

"There now, I won't hurt you," Peridot crooned. "Let me get you back to your mum."

The creature blinked its enormous eyes. Peridot wished she could see their color, but they looked like pools of black in the darkened tent. "That's right," she whispered. "I'm here to help you."

Something in her tone relaxed the creature, and it let her reach into the cage and pull it free. She wrapped her arms around the baby, alarmed by the tremors that wracked its tiny body.

"Shhhh." She bounced and rocked it, trying to soothe its fears. "You're safe now."

The shaking continued, though Peridot convinced herself it diminished a bit. "Let's go," she whispered to Simran.

He held the flap open and she ducked into the moonlit camp outside. She paused in the bright light from the campfire and the nearly-full moon overhead, searching for Bryoni, who she'd expected to see just outside the tent. Kent's eyes went wide at the sight of the dragonet in her arms and he accepted the bow and quiver from Simran without acknowledging the exchange.

Peridot's pulse kicked up a notch as she searched the shadows for Bryoni. Between the middle and right tents, something moved in the darkness. Peridot squinted and leaned forward, trying to get a better look. A faint orange glow lit the area, and Peridot sighed in relief. Bryoni crouched between the tents, though Peridot couldn't see what she was doing.

Clutching the baby in her arms, Peridot rushed over to her friend. Soft crunching in the dirt told her that Kent and Simran stayed close on her heels.

She passed the fire and the dragonet made a purring noise. Hungry. The baby was hungry. She must have smelled the poachers' food. The pans sat empty and dirty on the ground beside the fire.

"We'll get you something to eat as soon as we can," Peridot murmured.

"Look, he's alive!" Bryoni crouched next to a wolf's still form between the tents. "Can you heal him here? He won't let me move him."

Peridot crouched down beside the animal and pressed a hand to his heaving chest. The wolf whimpered but laid his head on the ground. Peridot focused the energy, trying to keep as much light away from the tents as she could. After several moments, the wolf made a soft chuffing noise and stood. Peridot watched as he limped off into the shadows.

When she couldn't see him anymore, she shifted the

baby in her arms and stood. She carried the dragonet through the camp, away from the tents, and into the forest beyond. Leaves crunched behind her as her friends followed close behind. The infant dragon purred and chirped every few steps, and Peridot worried she'd wake the poachers. Above, something large followed their progress, rustling and cracking branches as it moved through the treetops.

They found a small clearing and Simran, Kent, and Bryoni ducked behind wide trees at the perimeter, but Peridot kept going. Her heart pounded in her throat, but she'd bet her life that the infant's mother was the one making all the noise in the treetops. No other animal would dare to make so much noise. She found an opening in the trees large enough for an adult dragon to land and set the infant in the center of the clearing. Before she could back away, the mother swooped down from above, screeching her fury and throwing fire at Peridot.

Peridot ducked and rolled away from the flames, and just managed to catch a glimpse of a second dragon carrying the infant away in the night.

"Wait," Peridot shouted at the dragon. Her hands shook, but she crouched behind a tree and pulled the eggs from the quiver slung over her shoulder. Each one was half as long as her forearm and weighed at least ten pounds, but she handled them as gently as if they were made of the finest porcelain. She stacked them carefully in front of her and backed away into the trees.

Another wave of fire swept toward her, but Peridot threw her arms in front of her face and stood her ground. She needed to see the mother take the eggs, though she couldn't explain why, even to herself. The enormous dragon chirruped and rumbled. She approached the tree as if Peridot were the dangerous one, grabbed one egg in each claw, and spread her wings wide. With a great gush of wind and happy rumbling, the dragon took to the air.

Peridot choked back a sob of happy relief. Those babies wouldn't grow up in the poachers' dangerous world.

Another wave of fire blasted her back, and Peridot stumbled, confused. She'd thought the only dragons had taken off with the infant and the eggs. Clearly, she'd been wrong. She ducked behind the nearest tree and made herself as small as she could manage, hoping the dragon wouldn't find her in the dark. It called and circled over-head, blowing occasional blasts of fire and smoke down into the forest near Peridot's hiding place. Finally, it gave one last angry call and flew off into the night sky.

Peridot relaxed but didn't leave her hiding spot just yet. She waited until the sound of the dragons' beating wings faded before she stood and made her way back to her friends.

"What happened? Is he dead?" She asked, approaching the spot where Simran lay motionless on the ground.

"No. He's breathing." Kent gathered a bunch of leaves and shoved them under Simran's head. Blood soaked them in an instant from a wound Peridot couldn't see. "He's in bad shape, though. He tried to follow you, and one of the dragons…"

Peridot nodded and glanced at the moonlit sky. "I don't like this, but let's see what I can do."

She breathed in, drawing the mountain's power in through her feet until it pounded against her chest, demanding release. She focused first on Simran's dangerously depleted blood supply, replacing as much of it as she possibly could. His face flushed pink and returned to its normal color, the frightening pallor fading with each second. When she was satisfied that he had enough to fill his limbs and body, she moved her attention to his head. Since he couldn't tell her where his injuries were, she'd move from the top down.

Something clicked and snapped beneath Peridot's hands, and Simran gasped and opened his eyes. Pain and confusion filled his eyes, but she couldn't hold his gaze and heal him at the same time. She moved her hands to his neck. Nothing there seemed out of place, so she let her hands drift lower, caressing his chest and feeling for bruises and broken ribs. Nerves, tendons, and blood vessels crackled and popped back into their proper places beneath her healing touch. She focused on his injuries with every bit of energy she possessed.

"I'm going to climb and get a better look around," Bryoni murmured.

Peridot nodded but didn't take her attention off Simran.

Beneath her careful touch, Simran moaned and tried to roll away. Kent held the injured man's shoulders in place on the soft ground so Peridot could continue her work. She moved her hands to his arms but stopped short of trying to regrow the severed forearm. She just didn't have enough time for that. Every moment they spent in the clearing left them vulnerable to attack by dragons, wild animals, or worse, the poachers.

When his arms were mostly healed, she moved her hands to his legs. The right one had been broken again, in several places. She focused the light, breathing steadily to pull the energy from the mountain and channel it through her hands.

The femur made a loud pop and lifted under her hands as the bone reknit. Simran bit his lip against the pain and moaned softly.

"You have to keep quiet," Peridot murmured. She switched her attention to the other leg but found nothing more serious than bruises and a bit of swelling in his ankle. She fixed those and released him. He'd need a few minutes to catch his breath before he'd be able to walk.

"Um, Peridot?" Bryoni's whisper from above raised alarm bells in Peridot's mind.

"What is it?"

"The poachers. The dragons must have woken them up, and they know we're gone. They're checking around the camp now, but we don't have much time."

Peridot glanced down. Her patient had closed his eyes again, so she grabbed Simran's shoulders. "You have to get up, do you hear me? We have to go now, or they'll have us again."

Simran's eyes opened and he sat up.

Peridot held out a hand which Simran grabbed with his good arm. "You'll have to keep up. I'm not sure they'll be willing to save your neck again." She hoped he didn't see the weakness behind the threat. She knew she'd never be able to leave a living sprite, or any other creature, to face those poachers alone. Besides, if it hadn't been for him, she wouldn't have found the babies.

He wobbled a bit at first, found his feet, and took off through the forest after Bryoni and Kent. Peridot smiled at his determination and sprinted to the front of the group. She had the best chance of leading them to safety, though they'd have to avoid the wolves' den this time. She ran into a wide clearing and cursed softly. At least a dozen dragons circled overhead. Two by two, they dove toward her clearing.

"Go back! Find a tree and don't move," she screamed even as she took her own advice.

Footsteps crunched through the forest behind them, and Peridot's mind whirled. How could she get them out of this one? Could they climb? They'd have the advantage over the poachers from the branches above. No, Simran only had one hand. He wouldn't be able to climb.

An arrow whirred past her head, and Peridot resisted the urge to peek out around her tree. Since when did the poachers have arrows?

Heat exploded from the clearing, singeing her eyebrows and bringing tears to her eyes.

Somewhere beside her, Kent grunted softly and let out a moan. "Peri, I'm hit. Can you get to me?"

"Where are you?" She whispered.

He moaned again but didn't answer.

"Bryoni, can you see Kent?"

"No, I think he's close, though." Bryoni's whisper sounded rough and forced, and Peridot hoped she wasn't injured, too.

Peridot drew a breath and pulled in as much energy as

she dared. Her insides quivered. If she did this wrong, she and her friends wouldn't live to see the morning, let alone have a chance to warn the villagers about her father and the poachers.

The old man's voice spoke as if in her ear, and though she'd never heard the words before, she whispered them without considering what they might mean. She didn't think to look around for the man who'd showed them to the cave. A brilliant yellow light erupted from her hands, creating a column of light in the center of the clearing. The dragons circled the column, and the crunching footsteps behind her stopped.

"Heal your brother," the old man's voice carried on the breeze. "He is in trouble."

She didn't know where the voice came from, but she didn't waste time looking for it. The column of light shone brightly in the clearing, distracting the dragons above and lighting up the forest around it. Kent lay between two broad sycamore trees, sprawled on his face with an arrow sprouting from his shoulder.

Rocks, sticks, and roots caught her feet and tripped her as she ran to her brother, but she stumbled over them and kept going. His rapid, shallow breathing worried her.

She inhaled the mountain's power even before she reached him. She fell to her knees beside him, pressed her hands into his back, and exhaled every wisp of power she held within her chest.

The power jolted Kent up off the ground, but he slumped over and didn't respond. Peridot shook him hard by the shoulders. Nothing happened. She drew in the power once more and pressed her hands to his back. Power flowed into him, but she couldn't seal the wound in his shoulder. Desperate, she yanked the arrow free. Something black and slimy oozed from the wound. Peridot leaned back, examining the poison.

"Help me," she whispered to the mountain. "Tell me how to fix this." She listened for words, like the ones that had appeared in her mind only a few minutes before. Only silence answered back.

Tears streamed down her face. She had to figure out how to save her brother. She tossed her head back and peered up into the night sky, willing the mountain or the forest or the dragons or the mysterious man to give her the key to helping Kent.

Strong hands gripped her shoulders. Peridot dropped her gaze from the sky to Bryoni's face.

"We have to move. They're almost here."

Peridot shook her head and tried again to use the power to heal the wound in her brother's shoulder. The harder she tried, the more foul black slime oozed out of the gash.

"Go," Peridot whispered with the last shred of energy she possessed. "Take Simran. Run to the village. Get help!"

Bryoni gasped. "No. I'm not leaving you here. I don't even know how to get back to the village or what to watch out for in the dark."

"Please. I need help if he's going to have any chance."

Kent gasped and jerked, and Peridot breathed in more of the mountain's power.

"You have to go." Her voice shook as much as her hands. She pressed her hands directly onto the wound and focused all her attention on directing the power into Kent. Light skittered over his skin and flowed into him. Once more, it had no effect.

She glanced up at Bryoni. "Please. Just follow the trails." She pointed the correct direction. "Run. Once you reach the edge of the forest, you'll be safe. Get help."

Peridot never would have imagined a scenario where she'd beg anyone to leave her alone in the forest at night, but this wasn't something she could have dreamed up in her worst nightmares.

Slowly, Bryoni nodded. "All right. Let's go." She grabbed Simran's arm and tugged, but he didn't budge.

"I don't think this is a good idea. We shouldn't leave them." He gestured to Peridot and Kent, his eyes wild.

"You heard her. We have to get help!" Bryoni tugged again, and Simran nodded. This time he let her pull him into motion, and they took off at a run.

The crunching of their footsteps faded into the dark, and Peridot fought a wave of hopelessness. She wished she could call Bryoni back.

"There!" The man's voice reached her through the trees, and Peridot stood and placed herself between her brother and the poachers.

"You've killed him," she wailed into the forest. Acting purely on instinct, she raised her hands and drew in the power. She murmured something that made no sense and watched as purple light flew from her hands at the poachers.

The night's aurora began as the faintest hint of blue and purple light through the trees. It grew brighter and brighter until the light blazed with as much force as the afternoon sun. Peridot squinted against the blinding light. She'd never seen it so bright before, but it didn't last. Within a few heartbeats, it faded out again, drifting in rivers of blue and purple and green over the mountain and through the trees.

As it died out, so did the purple light that held her enemies captive. A dragon screeched overhead, and the poachers fell toward the ground.

"I thought you were going to help me," she yelled at the mountain.

The poachers landed with a crash but didn't stay down. They leapt to their feet and ran toward her.

"We've got more of that for you, if you try to fight us." The man pointed to the black wound on Kent's back.

The same instant the poachers reached her, the mother dragon crashed through the trees behind her, screaming rage. Smoke plumes poured from her nose and mouth. Peridot froze, knowing any movement would draw the dragon's attention.

The poachers ran, scattering in different directions and drawing the dragons away from Peridot and her brother.

"Kent." She shook his shoulder as carefully as she could, doing her best not to move the injured area. "Can you hear me? We have to try to get away from here before they come back."

He groaned but didn't move.

A dragon screamed in pure fury. The rage in the sound brought goosebumps up on Peridot's arms and raised the little hairs at the back of her neck. A brilliant flash of fire lit the forest to her right. Panic filled her chest, but she pushed the feeling away and tried to remember what she'd learned about treating poisons.

Shouts of pain and fear echoed through the trees, breaking her focus for a heartbeat. Out of ideas, she breathed in again, pulling the energy into her chest. This time, she waited longer, drawing more power into herself with each breath until the light radiated from every pore. Her heart crashed against her ribs. She'd never held so much power before, and its wildness terrified her. Sweat beaded on her forehead despite the night's growing chill.

So much energy filled her chest that she struggled to draw breath. She bent over Kent and placed both hands on his shoulder, encircling the wound with her fingers.

"Sanitatem venenum." She hoped that was the right command, but she couldn't remember for sure. White light flashed, blinding in its intensity. The light surrounded Peridot and Kent, and the black ooze coming from the wound slowed. One agonizing millimeter at a time, the wound's edges pulled together.

Kent screamed and thrashed against her hands, but she held him in place. His cries pierced her heart. His pain became hers, and she trembled beneath its crushing weight. The light around them ebbed and dimmed. Peridot drew more power from the mountain, working to maintain the glow. When it faded more, she shouted the charm again.

The light flared. Kent screamed. His thrashing had more strength, and she had to use every ounce of energy she possessed to keep her hands on his shoulder. He raised his torso off the ground and shook to push her away.

"I'm sorry. I am, but you have to be still. Let me heal you." She shouted the words over his screams.

Another dragon's cry cut through her concentration. This one was closer, and pain mingled with the rage in the animal's call.

Peridot cursed under her breath. No more poison had come from the wound, but it still hadn't closed. Still, Kent's renewed strength gave her hope.

Fire flashed into the clearing behind her, its heat scorching her back.

Peridot flinched, stumbled, and lost her hold on her brother. The healing glow died, but Kent sat up.

"What'd you do? Light it on fire? That was awful. And it doesn't feel like it's gone." He moved his arm in a circle, testing its strength and mobility.

"It's not completely healed, but that poison was almost too much for me." She sniffed and wiped the tears from her cheeks. "I thought I was going to lose you."

Dragon calls mingled with a woman's scream behind her. "Do you think you can move? We need to go before they get any closer."

"I think so." He groaned and pushed himself to his feet. "Where's Bryoni? Simran?"

"I sent them for help."

The woman screamed again. Something snapped and crashed. The trees shook.

"Let's go." Peridot gathered up her bow and quiver from where Kent had dropped them, grabbed Kent's muddy linen sleeve, and pulled him with her into the trees. She ran toward the poachers' camp, hoping she'd be able to circle around and avoid both the dragons and the thieves.

*P*eridot ran around a huge sycamore tree and stopped cold. The last man in the poachers' group stood in the path, his hands on his knees. She didn't think he'd seen her, since he didn't look in her direction, but she couldn't see what he was so focused on. She squinted into the darkness, trying to make sense of the lump on the side of the trail in front of him.

Flames licked at the trail behind her, evidence that the dragons had nearly caught up. She ducked behind the tree, pulled out her bow and grabbed a handful of arrows. Exhaustion and fear dragged at her arms, making her clumsy. She dropped two arrows and bent to retrieve them. She almost dropped the bow but managed to clutch it to her chest as she straightened with the arrows in hand. She placed one against the bow string and assumed the stance that was as familiar as breathing, but she couldn't bring herself to shoot the man. He'd made no move toward her. In fact, he was so focused on the lump on the ground that he didn't seem to have seen her at all.

"I'm sorry," he yelled.

Peridot jumped and loosed the arrow at the unexpected sound. She hadn't aimed, and the arrow flew wild and landed harmlessly in a tree. The man didn't react.

"We should never have come here. You were right all along." He sniffed and wiped his face on his shirt.

"What do we do?" Kent whispered, his head close to Peridot's ear. "We can't stay here."

A dragon's call sounded so close behind Peridot that she expected to turn and see the beast breathing smoke in her face. Shaken, she glanced over her shoulder. Nothing. Where was it? It was nearly on top of them, judging by the sound of that cry.

Kent's eyes met hers in the darkness, and together they moved toward the man on the path. Careful to avoid any sticks or rocks that would alert him to their presence, they crept forward. Peridot struggled to control her breathing. Her pulse pounded in her ears, so loud she was sure the man would hear it. Her knees turned to rubber and she worried they'd fail to hold her up.

"Tarkhaan! Where are you? They're getting away!" A woman's voice froze Peridot in place.

"I don't care. Let them go." The despondence in the man's voice affected Peridot more than she would have believed possible. These sprites had tried to enslave her and her brother and her friends then had tried to kill them more than once and had nearly succeeded. She signaled to Kent, and they snuck off the trail and into the trees where they could hide until the poachers moved on.

"Look," the woman said. "We can still salvage this trip. Let's get the crystals and get off this mountain before the weakling and his new friend come back with help."

"We've lost the dragonet and the eggs. The slaves got away. What are we supposed to sell to even break even?"

"We'll wait at the camp until morning. By then, that dragon should be dead, and we can skin it for a trophy. And we have the wolves and eagles. Those should fetch a good price on their own. Just imagine if we really do get the crystals, though. That's enough to set us up for life. No more traveling. No more hunting. No more worrying. It's what she would have wanted."

Peridot stifled a gasp.

A dragon, dying? Where? I have to find it.

She'd heard one nearby. In her haste, she forgot she was hiding. She stood up and hurried off in the direction of the dragon's call.

"Hey!" The woman's shout split the quiet, and realization spread over Peridot like ice water. "Catch her!"

A curse word slipped out, louder than she'd ever dared before. Peridot sprinted to the other side of the trail and raised her bow. She nocked an arrow and spun to face the poachers. A loud crack beside her ear brought her up short.

When she lowered the bow and examined the smooth wood, she cursed again. A long crack ran the length of the grip. Her stomach twisted. She let one more curse fly and tossed the useless bow aside.

"Peri!" Kent reached her and grabbed the fringe on the front of her shirt. "We have to run!"

Peridot drew a breath and planted her feet firmly on the rocky soil. She drew another, deeper breath, as she had when working to save her brother, and concentrated on the charm she wanted to use. She licked her parched lips, her mouth suddenly dry as a desert. The energy swirled inside her—a torrent of power that could heal or destroy in equal measure.

"Murus ignis!" She couldn't muster much volume, but red light shot from her hands. She cursed again. A blazing wall of fire lit the path. Her breath left her in a rush. She'd gotten it wrong again. The fire trapped her between it and the poachers, instead of securing her escape.

"I swear, if we live through this, I'll go to lessons every single day."

Kent made a strangled squeal Peridot took as an agreement.

The two poachers bore down on them, eying the wall of fire as if it were a trap set for them.

Desperate, Peridot reached for her brother, clamped her fingers around his sleeve, and sprinted into the blackness of the forest. After only fifty paces, Peridot caught her foot on a root and sprawled in the dirt. The impact knocked the wind from her lungs, and she lay still, stunned and struggling for breath.

"Peridot! You have to get up. They're right behind me." Kent pulled her up and shoved her forward.

Pain shot through her chest, and air refused to fill her right lung. She gasped for breath, but only managed an odd gurgling sound. Peridot stopped and leaned against the nearest tree, trying to draw in enough of the mountain's energy to fix her chest, but only managed a faint glow. Something small closed within her. It would have to be enough.

The taste of blood filled her mouth and she spat. Peridot tried a tentative breath. Her left side expanded normally, but something still wasn't working on the right.

Kent grabbed her beneath her arms and pulled her between the trees. Behind them, footsteps crunched on the rocky ground and crashed through the underbrush. Kent half-carried, half-dragged her along beside him, but the pressure of his arm on her chest was agony. Every breath hurt more than the one before it. Her vision swam, and blackness filled the periphery.

"I...I can't," she panted.

Kent lifted her feet off the ground and carried her for another twenty paces.

"Please. Please stop. I need a rest."

He slowed his steps and eased her to the ground behind a broad tree. Her breath came in shallow gasps punctuated by wet, raspy coughs that felt like knives slicing through her chest. Dimly, she wished the mountain would do something to help, but the odd man didn't appear, and no unexpected powers manifested in her body. Waves of fatigue and weakness washed over her. It took all her strength to stay sitting up against the tree.

"What can I do?" Kent knelt beside her and brushed her long hair out of her face.

Peridot couldn't muster the energy to answer. Instead, she focused on the mountain. Her shallow breaths couldn't draw much of its power, but tiny wisps of light pushed back the blackness swimming in front of her eyes. She blocked out everything else. Nothing mattered but that light. Not the poachers. Not the dragons. Not even her brother, who was easily her favorite sprite in the world. Only the light could save her. If it healed her, she could help the others.

Each breath made her stronger. She couldn't say how

much time passed, but eventually her breaths grew deeper and less painful.

"Can you go on? I don't think we have much time." Kent's anxious whisper drew Peridot back to the present.

She pressed her fingers against the tender spot on her chest. It stayed put and didn't impede her breathing. Encouraged, she nodded. "I think so."

He pulled her to her feet, and she paused, testing her breath and waiting to make sure the dizziness didn't return.

It didn't.

Triumph reigned for an instant, followed immediately by panic. The poachers' footsteps ground into the dirt nearby, so close Peridot worried they'd capture her and Kent again.

Peridot stood frozen, afraid to move and alert the poachers to her presence. She'd already made that mistake once.

When the noise faded into the darkness in the thickening wood, Peridot and Kent crept into the forest in the opposite direction.

A dragon's pained bleat stopped her in her tracks. Right. She'd come this way to find and help the dragon the murdering poachers had injured. Kent pulled her away, toward the path and safety, but she refused to move.

"I have to try to heal it."

Peridot measured every step, careful to avoid any sticks or pebbles that would sound the alarm. It was slow going, but she followed the dragon's weakening calls.

Kent said nothing, but he paused every three or four steps to peer over his shoulders. No sounds announced the poachers' location, though Peridot knew they were close by. They may have stopped to rest or could be creeping just as quietly through the forest behind Peridot and Kent.

LAST STAND

In the darkness, Peridot missed the gentle downslope and stumbled. She would have fallen again, but Kent grasped her elbow and steadied her. The trees thinned, and Peridot slowed, keeping to the shadows around trees wide enough to hold three sprites abreast. Wide branches spread overhead, blocking out great swaths of moonlight and providing shadows dark enough to hide them.

Dark enough to hide a dragon.

Peridot didn't see the animal at first. She tripped on its twitching tail and ran a few steps to keep on her feet.

The dragon bellowed and swung its clubbed tail after her.

"Shhhh. It's all right." She ducked under another swing of the massive tail. "I'm here to help you."

Another swing. This one brushed the hair at her cheek. Peridot dodged away, moving toward the animal's back where it wouldn't be able to strike her. She hoped she could calm it before it had a chance to cook her with its fire breath.

Fear renewed her strength and lent quickness to her steps. She drew in the mountain's power, hoping against hope that the man had been right when he'd said the mountain loved her. She needed its love and help now more than she ever had before.

Power filled her, overflowing her chest and swirling in her abdomen and arms. She pressed her hands to the dragon's back, just below where its wings attached, and let the light flow from her and into the bleating beast. She whispered the charm almost without thinking and waited.

Light blazed in the clearing, illuminating the iridescent green scales coated in black slime. Peridot groaned. The poison. That was the same poison that had nearly taken Kent from her.

The fire of her hope dimmed but refused to go out completely. She had saved Kent. She could—no, she *would* —save this dragon.

Power soared in her chest. Green light blinded her. The dragon thrashed and tried to roll over.

"Over here! I'm here!" Kent shouted, drawing the dragon's attention away from her.

Peridot pulled in everything the mountain would give her with every breath. She held none of it. Every shred of energy that coursed through her feet passed directly into the wounded, screaming dragon. She was nothing but a conduit between the source of all power and the animal it healed.

A new, high-pitched howl threatened to break Peridot's concentration, but she blocked it out. It wasn't important. All that mattered was cleansing the poison from the dragon's enormous body. Peridot opened her eyes and stared at the creature that towered over her. Even lying on its side, it was at least four times her height, at least that was her best guess since she barely reached halfway to the spiny ridge of its backbone.

"Peridot! Look out!"

The call brought her head up, but she refused to take her hands from the dragon. It had stopped thrashing and now lay still, howling like an angry wildcat at the pain the poison caused.

At the last second, she saw the reason for Kent's warning: the light had drawn the poachers. The man stood with his bow pulled tight, a dripping arrow pointed squarely at Peridot's back.

"So, you're a healer," he sneered. "That explains so much. Now, what has to happen for you to heal my wife? This thing nearly cut her leg off, and she's dying on the path back there."

Peridot shook her head, but kept her hands fixed to the dragon. "I can't. I can only heal the mountain's creatures."

"You lie," the woman said through gritted teeth. "You healed the weakling, didn't you?" She paused, considering. "Twice."

"The mountain accepted him. If it hadn't, he would have died that first night. The wolves wouldn't have allowed him into their home."

"What do I do to make the mountain accept her?" The man's voice had lost its venom. Now he sounded on the brink of begging.

Kent stepped between Peridot and the arrow. "You fools. You've killed, maimed, and imprisoned so many of the mountain's most loved ones there's no way it will allow its power to heal one of your number."

Peridot shot Kent a grateful glance. She'd worried he wouldn't catch on in time to avoid blowing her lies wide open. "Besides that, I'm not even that good of a healer." Peridot struggled to maintain the glow around the dragon while keeping her eyes on the poachers. Sweat beaded on her lip and dripped down her back. Her legs shook and her lungs burned with the effort.

"I see what you're doing." The man sounded furious. "You're trying to keep me talking long enough so you can revive that thing, then you'll let it kill us both so you can run free. Well, it won't work. You're coming with me, and you're going to save my wife or die trying."

The poachers stalked closer, and Kent spread his arms and flailed them wildly—to block any attempt at an arrow shot, Peridot guessed.

The dragon's howl took on a new, frantic note. The pitch stabbed at Peridot's ears, drowning out all other thoughts. What she could see of the wounds on the dragon's back were mostly closed, though one still oozed black, sticky slime. She wished she knew for sure how many times the poachers had shot the creature. It was amazing they hadn't run out of arrows.

Someone grabbed her shoulder. Peridot closed her eyes. Bryoni had done something that burned the ropes off her wrists and arms.

"Help me," she murmured, too quietly for anyone to hear over the dragon's scream. "Cutis Ignis," she whispered. Her eyes popped open in shock. She'd never heard that charm before, but a soft orange glow emanated from her leather shirt and exposed skin.

The man screamed and the hand on her shoulder sizzled. He released her and fell backward in his scramble to escape her flaming skin.

"No," Kent shouted.

He doubled over, clutching at his belly. The woman stood in front of him, a sword in her hands. Bright red blood dripped from the blade.

Peridot gasped, but kept her hands glued to the dragon's smooth back.

"You're coming with us." The woman brandished the sword. "You'll heal my sister if you want to have time to come back and save your brother."

Eyes wide, Peridot shook her head. Even if she'd wanted to, she didn't think she could make it back to the woman. Her legs trembled and barely supported her weight. Her lungs ached. Exhaustion, dehydration, and the gnawing pain of hunger warred for the last shred of her concentration.

"You'll have to bring her here." Peridot couldn't muster a voice above a whisper. She hoped they'd be able to hear over the dragon's vocalizations. "I'm too weak to walk to her."

The man stepped back, but the woman refused. "No. You'll be gone by the time we return. You come with us, or your brother dies."

Peridot shook her head and sweat ran off the end of her nose. "I couldn't if I wanted to. If my brother dies, he returns to the mountain that bore him. We would celebrate the end of his trials."

A new sound joined the dragon's anguished cries. This one chilled Peridot to her bones and made her long to run as far away as her legs could carry her, though it was unlike any sound she'd ever heard on the mountain before.

The woman screamed, her voice joining the dragon's and the new siren echoing through the predawn darkness outside the tiny circle of light. She raised her sword and ran at Peridot, her eyes unfocused and filled with rage.

The tip of the sword pierced Peridot just below her shoulder blade and glanced off her rib, but searing pain burned through the muscle and bone near the weapon's cut.

"You refuse to help my sister. Fine. Heal yourself or die like the animal you protect." Cold hatred sounded in the woman's voice.

Peridot swooned but struggled to keep her hands on the dragon's back. It was almost healed. No more blackness oozed from the wounds, though several were still raw and open.

Everything around her spun, and nausea stole the hunger and thirst she'd felt only a heartbeat before.

A curtain of red covered her vision. Her legs gave out. For the first time since she'd begun, her hands fell away from the dragon. She tried to apologize to the creature, but her tongue stuck to the roof of her mouth and refused to make the words.

She crumpled to the ground beside the green beast, barely aware of the fading light around her. She didn't know if the woman had given her an extra amount of the poison, or if her exhausted state made her more susceptible to it, but within a few breaths, her heart raced in her chest and sweat drenched the ground beneath her.

Something large shifted nearby, and the noise that had filled the air since she'd first entered the clearing cut off.

The silence rang like a bell in Peridot's mind, but she couldn't figure out why it mattered.

Heat erupted all around her, drying the sweat from her face and heating her more within her heavy leather clothes. She longed to pull them off but lacked the strength to move.

Someone screamed. The smell of burning hair and roasting meat made Peridot retch, and she choked on the effort of breathing after the heaving finished.

"Peridot?" Kent sounded like he was talking to her through a wall of water. "Peri?"

He held her arm and rolled her to her back. The movement set fire to her skin, and she stifled a scream. It escaped as a strangled moan.

"Can you help her?"

A soft rumbling sound seemed to answer him.

Something strong but intensely gentle wrapped around her torso and her hips. Air rushed past her, whipping her hair away from her face. Peridot tried to open her eyes, but the spinning, swirling images refused to make any sense. Panic fluttered at the edge of her awareness.

Kent? Kent what's happening? Her mouth didn't work. She moaned, but the words wouldn't come.

Light grew behind her eyelids, but she resisted the urge to look again. The last time had made her so dizzy. The wind on her face felt good, though, like standing at the edge of a cliff on a windy day and enjoying the view of the valleys below.

HOME

Something changed. The ground rushed up to meet her, but that didn't make any sense.

I'm on the ground, aren't I? No, I wasn't. But now I am. Did I fall asleep in a tree?

She struggled to remember. She had been doing something incredibly important, but what?

"Kent! Peridot! Get away from there!" Her mother's voice broke through the haze, but not fully. "They'll kill you. Back! Back, you big ugly beast."

"No, mother." That was Kent. "They're here to help—and to get help. Where's Evanora? We need her."

"I'm here," a small voice answered. "What's happened? You're bleeding."

Kent coughed and groaned. "I'll be all right with a little help, but Peridot's in trouble. She's been poisoned."

"Poisoned? By who?" Her mother sounded near hysterics. "Who would have poisoned her?"

Something touched the center of the fire on her back. Peridot screamed and struggled to escape.

"I see. Can you give me a little room?"

Brilliant white light enveloped Peridot. The ground fell away and hovered a few inches below her. At first, pain seared through every muscle and bone, but a heartbeat later, her entire body went numb. She couldn't breathe, she couldn't think, and she couldn't struggle.

Her mind strained against the healer's paralysis. *I need to fight. I've been fighting. Fighting who?* The numbness seeped in, replacing the panic and allowing the exhaustion to take over. Her face relaxed, and she drifted into a restless slumber.

SOMETHING HARD—A rock? No, it felt more like a stick—poked into her head. She frowned and reached for her favorite quilt. She wasn't ready to wake up yet. Her fingers reached for the end of her bed but tangled in something long and stringy. The blankets had gone missing, somehow.

Her eyes blinked open and fear coursed through her. She lay on the ground in tall grass. Dozens of people stood over her wearing expressions of fear and anxiety, lit by the first blush of dawn.

The events of the previous days flooded back into her mind and she sat upright, struggling to get to her feet.

"The poachers. They'll be here any minute." She searched the crowd for Kent. His face had none of its usual color, and he looked like a stiff wind would blow him over. The memory of the poacher stabbing him with her sword flashed through Peridot's still-slow mind. She turned to Evanora and met the elderly sprite's gentle green eyes.

"Thank you. Can you help him, too? They stabbed him."

"Peri, you can do it yourself. You've already healed me several times." Kent staggered toward her and seated himself at her feet. "I'm ready."

"No, let Evanora do it. I have so much left to learn. She knows how to numb the pain while the power heals you." Tears filled Peridot's eyes. How much better could she have done if she'd only listened to her friends and family? She'd learned so much in two days, what could she manage if she went to lessons every day?

Kent didn't argue but lay back on the ground and pulled up his blood-soaked tunic. Evanora stepped closer and whispered a soft command. Light surrounded Kent as the old woman worked. Peridot couldn't focus for long, so she let her eyes wander over the crowd.

Bryoni stood beside Simran, who waved with a fully restored hand and grinned at her. Peridot almost smiled back, but she wasn't entirely sure the danger had passed, yet.

The village gate swung open and Lord Maksym strode toward the crowd, his expression thunderous. All her father's scheming flowed through her mind, and Peridot turned away from the local lord. She'd have time to sort out what he knew and whether he had made her father work with the poachers later. She searched every face, looking for any sign of her father. She couldn't wait to confront him about what he'd said and done with the poachers.

A disjointed thought popped into her mind. *What happened with the last two poachers?*

They had wanted her to heal the one the dragon had

hurt. She remembered that much. When she'd refused, the woman had stabbed her with a poisoned sword.

Instinctively, she scanned the area for the poachers. They could be anywhere in the tall grasses.

Her gaze paused on an enormous dragon hovering behind the villagers. When the beast saw her looking, it hopped backward, showing her a much smaller dragon lying on the ground. Green blood oozed from numerous cuts along the young dragon's blue scales.

A tiny gasp escaped Peridot, and she turned away from Evanora and Kent and moved toward the dragons.

"Peridot! Stay here. A mother dragon with an injured baby is the most dangerous animal you've ever heard of." Her mother's sharp command stopped her.

Peridot shook her head. "No, mother. I'm the only one they'll let help them, though I know Evanora could do a better job. I…I think they trust me."

"You won't go anywhere near that dragon," Lord Maksym roared. "I forbid it. You'll bring those beasts down on all of us."

The old bitterness rose in her throat, but Peridot swallowed it. She had to know what he knew, but he'd never talk to her if she gave him nothing but barbs. "I'm sorry, my lord, but… they brought me here, didn't they?" She looked to the crowd for confirmation. Several villagers nodded, their eyes wide as saucers.

"And that mother carried her baby down here for me to heal, didn't she?"

More nods, and a few murmured, "she sure did."

Peridot turned back to Lord Maksym. "That mother thinks I can save her baby, and I probably can. I have to at least try."

When it looked like Lord Maksym was about to deny her again, she raised her hand and gestured to the dragons. "Imagine how much better life could be if the dragons trusted us, if they didn't attack every time we accidentally got too close. This could be the first step toward a life of peace with them."

"Well, I can't argue against that." Lord Maksym pressed his lips into a firm line and glared at her. "If this doesn't work and they come after us, I'm holding you personally responsible."

"That's fair," Peridot whispered. Fear clutched at her throat, but she walked away from the local lord and the rest of the crowd.

She strode through the tall grass toward the dragon, her hands held out to the sides and trailing through the grassy strands.

At her approach, the mother dragon made a soft chirrup and settled onto the ground behind the baby. Peridot knelt beside the bleeding dragonet. She was roughly twice the size of the one Peridot had carried out of the poachers' camp. Her leathery wings hung in tatters, limp against the soft ground. The baby's eyes were closed, and ragged, rattling breaths moved her chest up and down. The scales that should have laid in even, smooth rows instead looked ruffled like a bird's feathers after a rainstorm. Soft moans of pain and fear escaped with every breath. Tears filled Peridot's eyes at the trust the mother gave her.

"I'm not the best person for this," she whispered, "but I'll do everything I can."

She closed her eyes and breathed in deep—amazed for an instant that no pain accompanied the movement of her ribs. Energy filled her, stronger than ever, and she drew as much power as her tired, weak body could hold. Green light flowed from her hands when she laid them on the dragon's back. She whispered the charm, and brilliance enveloped Peridot and the dragon, lighting up the field and illuminating the side of the mountain. Peridot focused all her energy on the wounds, watching as one after another stopped bleeding, and the skin beneath reknit. The scales around the cuts slowly rearranged themselves into neat rows once more. The baby cried out once, but the mother pressed her face close to the frightened juvenile and made a soft purring sound.

Heat filled her feet and legs as Peridot channeled the mountain's power into the baby. Each time the little dragon cried out, Peridot tried another charm to see if she could figure out how to numb the pain. She wished she could remember what Evanora had said before Peridot's mind and body had gone numb.

The baby screamed as her wings reknit. The sound tore at Peridot's heart. She couldn't bear to cause so much pain to such an innocent creature. "Please help me, just one more time," she whispered. Tears flowed down her face unchecked.

"Reliqua pacificae." The wind whispered the words, and she said them aloud without a thought.

The baby relaxed and rested her head on her mother's outstretched paw. Pain left her body, and the baby closed her eyes and sighed deeply.

"Thank you," Peridot cried. "I promise I'll do better now. I'll learn all I can so I can help your creatures."

All the smaller wounds took a long time to close. The sun rose higher in the sky, trying hard to blind Peridot with its intensity. Finally, she searched the baby's skin and found no more injuries. All the scales lay flat and neat in orderly rows as they were supposed to. Peridot drew more power into her body and channeled it to the baby. She needed to replenish all the blood that had oozed out into the dirt, so much that the earth had turned to a thick, black mud beneath Peridot's feet. The baby's breathing evened out as her body remade the blood and cells it needed to thrive.

Weakness flooded Peridot's limbs, and she dropped her hands away from the sleeping dragonet. Unable to support herself, she fell back and sat on the ground. Grit filled her eyes, but she blinked them clear.

The mother dragon nuzzled the baby's face and made soft, soothing chirps and calls. Slowly, the baby opened her eyes and stared up into her mother's loving face. The moment was as tender and sweet as any Peridot had witnessed between a mother sprite and her child.

When the baby sat up and stretched her wings, Peridot stifled a cheer. Behind her, the villagers weren't so considerate. Applause and shouts of joy rang out, echoing across the grassy valley and bouncing back from the cliffs.

Peridot smiled and brushed her long, purple hair out of her eyes. She had so much to do, but first she needed a good meal and a bath and a few hours in her bed. She pushed herself to her feet, though the muscles in her legs protested.

The mother dragon made a strange chirrup that Peridot hadn't heard before. She raised her head and met the dragon's eyes. The happiness there brought tears back to Peridot's eyes. She didn't bother to fight them.

Another soft chirrup. This one, Peridot understood. It

was the dragons' sound of gratitude. She'd heard it before when she'd helped them move a fallen tree when it had trapped the juveniles in the lowest den.

Peridot grinned at the mother and nodded. "You're welcome. Thank you for letting me help her."

She turned to make the trek back to her family, but the dragon called her once more. Frowning, Peridot returned to the dragons. "What is it? Are you hurt, too?" She didn't really expect a reply, but her eyes skimmed the large dragon's even scales and found no sign of injury.

The dragon beat her wings against the air, raising a few feet off the ground. She flew a hundred yards back toward the mountain and dropped to the ground there.

Peridot frowned. *Maybe the mother is injured. Why's she staying so low? Maybe she's waiting for the baby to meet her there, to make sure she can fly.* Peridot glanced over at the baby, but the little one didn't move. Unsure what to do next, Peridot watched the dragons and waited. She'd healed the baby; she was sure of that much.

After a few moments of bouncing around in the grass, the mother dragon took flight once more. She returned and landed close beside the baby, in front of Peridot. She had something clutched in her right front claw, but Peridot couldn't see what it was. Horror doused her joy at healing the baby.

Is it one of the eggs the poachers stole? Did they injure it? They had looked whole to Peridot when she'd gathered them, but she hadn't had much light or time to examine those eggs. Her whole body tensed, but her muscles didn't have the strength to maintain the tension.

REST

The mother dragon hopped closer and loomed over her, but Peridot didn't have the energy to be afraid. Even if she had, she knew the mother wouldn't harm her. The dragon placed something at Peridot's feet, made a bowing motion with her long, graceful neck, and stretched her wings out. An instant later, she was high in the air circling above the villagers and calling out in happiness. The baby joined her mother in the sky a heartbeat later.

Peridot shielded her eyes from the sun and watched the rest of the dragons fly over to meet the pair. Together, the flight of dragons vanished into the mountain's protective caves.

When she couldn't see the dragons anymore, Peridot lowered her gaze to see what the mother had left. An opaque white crystal the size of her calf lay at her feet. It glowed softly in the morning sun. Peridot's breath caught in her throat. This was one of the crystals her father had been willing to kill for. Some sprites believed they were the source of the mountain's power, but Peridot agreed with what the one poacher had said—the power stemmed from the land itself.

Still, the crystal was worth more than anything Peridot had ever owned. There was no denying the power that coursed through her when she bent down and picked it up. Its weight surprised her, and she dropped it once before she managed to stand up with it.

She cradled it like a baby and trudged back toward the assembled villagers.

Fatigue shook her legs and weighed down her eyelids. She had to shift the crystal's weight every ten paces or so to keep from dropping it. Her mother met her halfway between the spot where the baby's blood had soaked the dirt and the crowd of onlookers.

"Are you all right? I've never seen you move so slow."

Peridot bit back a sigh. "I'm just very tired, Mother. It's been a long few days."

"I didn't know what had become of you." Her mother sniffed and wiped her face. "When Kent didn't come home and then you and Bryoni vanished before dawn, I feared the worst. Your father told everyone the dragons had caught you—that you'd finally gotten too close."

At the mention of her father, Peridot stiffened. "Mother—"

Her mother's shoulders drooped, and a sheen of tears clouded her eyes. "I already know. Bryoni told me your father tried to have you killed. When he heard Bryoni had returned home, he claimed he was going to find you and Kent and left again. I don't suppose he'll return now."

"I'm sorry, Mother." Peridot grunted and shifted the

crystal again. She should cry, too, she thought. Maybe she was just too tired.

"Why are you sorry? I can't tell you how happy I am to have you home. Here. That looks heavy." Her mother took the crystal and carried it a few steps. "What is this, anyway? I mean, I know what it is, I think, but why do you have it?"

"The mother dragon gave it to me. It's a gift for helping her baby."

"A gift from a dragon." Awe filled her mother's raw voice, and goosebumps grew on Peridot's arms. "That's incredible. I'm so proud of you. Bryoni told me you kept them all alive up there."

Peridot shook her head. "I realized how little I really know. I've decided to start going to lessons every day. I'll need more training if I ever want to be able to really help, like Evanora does."

"You're young yet, child. You have years ahead of you to learn as much as you want to know. Here, you should carry this into the village." She handed the crystal back to Peridot.

They didn't speak as they entered the crowd. Her mother led Peridot straight through the assembly and only paused long enough to open the tall iron gates. She took her daughter and son home, where they had a hearty breakfast of eggs and porridge. Once she'd eaten her fill, Peridot barely kept her eyes open long enough to trudge to her bed and collapse on top of the blankets.

RAISED voices brought Peridot out of a deep slumber.

Bleary and sleepy, it took her several long minutes before she placed the voices, and even longer before she could decipher their words.

"She needs to be better managed," a deep voice said. "What other woman would take off into the forest for days on end in a crazy chase like that?"

"I think you've misunderstood what happened." Kent's voice sounded furious, though he kept the volume low. "Those poachers captured me in our very own garden. Peridot followed the tracks and found me."

"I understand that, the love of a brother and all, but she put my baby girl in the gravest danger possible."

"No, mother. I didn't have to go with her." A long pause. "Really. She tried to talk me into staying, but I didn't want her to go alone."

"Nonsense. She goes up that mountain alone nearly every day."

"Yes, but she'd run into a few signs of trouble already. She told me all about the wounded wolves and the disappearing animals."

"Regardless, she should have gotten the adults. What would make a seventeen-year-old sprite think she can take on something like that on her own?"

Peridot rolled out of bed and stumbled to the curtain that separated her room from the main room. "Do I have a say in this?" The words sounded harsh, even to her own ears. She cleared her throat and softened her tone. "Look, in hindsight, I should have told someone we were going, but I'm sort of glad I didn't. I probably would have told Father, and he was one of them all along."

"She's got a point," Kent said. "Father probably would have 'looked for me' the same way he did when we didn't come home. And then I'd be sold to the highest bidder to a shipping company on the coast."

"Really, Hyacin." Peridot's mother plunked her mug down on the sturdy plank table. "I understand you're upset. We all are. But what if they hadn't gone? What then? You would just have poachers and slavers run loose in our forest?"

"Of course not. The adults should have handled it." Bryoni's father growled and downed the rest of his tea, and his eyes bored into Peridot's. "Why didn't you come get us at once?"

"Well, sir, when I went looking for him, I assumed he'd gotten lost. If I had known there were poachers and slavers in the forest, I would have gotten someone more competent than myself to go after them. Bryoni's skill saved our necks more than once."

"But my daughter says you'd noticed signs of trouble before then." Hyacin frowned, delicate lines appearing between her soft green eyes.

"I did, but I thought it was one of the twins robbing my traps again. I had no reason to think strangers were looking for sprites to kidnap."

"Exactly," Peridot's mother slapped her palm on the table. "It's preposterous to expect them to guess at something like that. We've never had any kind of trouble like this before."

"I will concede that point." Bryoni's father rubbed his temples.

"Look, this has been a tough few days for all of us. I'm just happy to have all our kids back in the village, safe and sound." Fatigue and strain showed on Lorenza's face.

Everyone voiced their agreement.

Hyacin stood and shot a tired glance at Peridot. "Well, since that's settled, let's get home to our own family, shall we?"

Bryoni and her father stood and strolled to the door.

"I'll see you tomorrow, all right?" Bryoni waved to Peridot, who smiled and waved back.

Peridot dropped into the seat her best friend had vacated. "How long was I asleep?"

"Most of the day, but that's all right." Peridot's mother set a steaming mug of berry tea on the table. "You needed to rest a bit. We do have a lovely surprise for you, though."

"Besides this lovely tea, you mean?" Peridot wrapped her fingers around the mug and brought it to her lips. The warmth seeped into her hands and welcomed her home more effectively than any gift could.

Kent laughed and sipped his own drink. "I know what you mean. I'd started to wonder if I'd ever be warm again."

"If I'd known you'd be so easy to please after such an ordeal, I'd have hired thugs to hide in the forest years ago." Angene had been so quiet in her spot on the other side of the sitting room that Peridot hadn't noticed her presence before that moment.

"I'm sure you enjoyed being an only child—even if it was only for a few days," Peridot shot back. The old animosity annoyed her now that she realized how petty it was, so she tried again. "I'm sorry. I shouldn't snap at you. I guess coming that close to losing everything was enough to make me rethink my normal behavior." She paused and added, "Why *are* you so awful to me all the time? What have I done to make you hate me so much?"

Angene made a face. "Your weirdness means none of the young men want anything to do with me. You're perfectly happy to tromp through the woods all the time with no thought of how your behavior affects your family's standing in town. Like I'm supposed to be a spinster so you can play with the wolves."

Stung, Peridot flushed. "Well, I—"

"As I was saying," her mother interrupted. "Lord Maksym and his nephew have agreed to join us for supper tonight. His niece decided all the excitement was too much for her and has taken the coach back home."

Peridot's stomach fell, but she tried to force a smile. "That's right. They were supposed to come the other day. How did that go?"

"It didn't. The nephew's carriage from the plains was robbed. He and several others were kidnapped. They thought he was dead." Peridot's mother bowed her head as if mourning. "It was quite a shock to everyone when he showed up with Bryoni."

Peridot blinked. "You mean Simran? He's Lord Maksym's nephew?" She gripped her mug tighter as all the warmth left her.

"Yes! No one could believe how beat up he looked. Of course, Evanora got him all fixed up, but he refused to go to his uncle's house. Of course, now that we know your father," she paused and swallowed hard before continuing, "your father was working with the poachers, we all understand why. Of course, it just made sense for them to both come here for supper so we can all hear the whole story."

None of her mother's ramblings made sense to Peridot. "Mother, slow down. If Simran hasn't gone to his uncle's house, how are they supposed to come here together?" The memory of Simran's face when Kent had suggested going to Lord Maksym for help flashed in Peridot's mind. Had Simran suspected his uncle even then?

Keeping her eyes on her empty mug, Peridot mumbled, "How do we know Lord Maksym wasn't the one who told Father to hire them?"

"Well, we don't. That's why I wanted him to come here with all of you, so you can catch him in any lies."

"Well, that makes sense, I guess." Kent plunked his empty mug down on the table. "Mother, could I have a bit more of that tea?"

THE HOT BATH her mother drew for her was the most luxurious thing Peridot had ever experienced. She only hoped her mother wasn't about to make the formal announcement of Peridot's courtship with Lord Maksym. The two had been left to scheme alone for three whole days—a fact that deeply concerned Peridot.

When the water cooled, she dried off and dressed in a comfortable day dress. She briefly considered the ugly gown she usually wore for Lord Maksym's visits, but the thought of Simran seeing her in that awful frock changed her mind. Instead, she settled for something simple and blue that set off her purple hair and made her brown eyes look more vibrant.

She couldn't help thinking of that morning in the city and her agreement to a courtship with Simran. So much had happened since then. She wasn't sure he'd be a good choice for her, given how impulsive he'd been on the mountain. She sighed and pushed the thought out of her mind. If he was truly Lord Maksym's nephew, he'd be expected to court Angene.

For some reason, the thought of the two of them together brought a surge of churning anger into her chest. She shook it off and ran a comb through her long purple hair. It had taken her half an hour to wash all the leaves and twigs out of her hair, so she ran the comb through it again to make sure she hadn't missed any. A quick glance in the mirror showed her looking as good as she thought possible without spending hours on her hair, so she left the dressing room and took her place in the sitting room with her family.

The waiting was agony. Peridot relived every detail of the three days she'd spent with Simran in the forest. He'd tried to take over more than once and had endangered all of them with his rash decisions. But he'd also made her smile, and he'd led her to the baby dragon. Besides that, it was hard to forget the way energy had zinged between them whenever they touched.

"What are you scowling so hard at?" Kent's voice brought an end to her reverie.

Heat flooded her cheeks, and Peridot couldn't think of a suitable reply. A knock at the door saved her.

Peridot forced herself to stay sitting while her mother answered the door and ushered Simran into the sitting room. His pale green hair shone in the lamplight, amplified by the smart black leather suit he wore. His soft brown eyes met Peridot's across the room, and her heart did a little flip.

"It's good to see you again. You look really, um, nice." His voice cracked at the end and Peridot suppressed a smile.

"Please come in. Have a seat. Make yourself at home." Peridot winced at the stiff, ridiculous, greeting, but she pushed onward. "It's good to see you, too. I'm glad Evanora fixed your arm."

Simran flexed the fingers on the new hand. "So am I."

The conversation died, and Peridot turned to knotting and twisting her fingers in her lap. She wished she had gotten out her embroidery to work on. Bryoni's birthday was only a day away now, and she'd never be able to finish it before the party.

"I think your uncle should be here soon," Angene piped in. The syrupy sweetness of her voice and demeanor made Peridot want to puke. "Did you know I'm the one your uncle was bringing you here to meet?"

Peridot jerked her head up, anxious to see Simran's response.

"Really? That's very interesting. It's a shame so much of the plan went so wrong."

Angene's face fell at the lack of interest in Simran's face and voice. He didn't even take his eyes off Peridot to answer her. A tiny thrill of triumph rose in her throat, but Peridot tried to hide it.

Another knock at the door brought the brief conversation to an end. Once more, Peridot's mother made the short trek to the door and held it open. Lord Maksym swept into the house without waiting for an invitation. If everyone else had made an attempt to clean up for the occasion, Lord Maksym looked to have done the opposite. His faded blue hair stuck up in wild disarray. Dark circles ringed his eyes. Dust and dirt covered his torn brown day suit.

To their credit, none of the sprites waiting in the cozy

room said anything about Lord Maksym's appearance, though Peridot had to bite her tongue hard to keep herself quiet.

Simran stood. "What's happened, Uncle? Are you injured?"

"I am well." Lord Maksym dragged his feet across the room and dropped into the chair Peridot's father had always occupied.

A pang of hurt and longing hit Peridot when she realized he'd never fill that seat again.

Lord Maksym waited until Peridot met his eyes. "I've just come from a meeting with your father."

Peridot struggled to keep her features impassive. "So, you *are* working with him?"

"No. No. Not in this." The bedraggled lord dropped his head into his hands and heaved a great sigh. "Your father's been a great worker for many years, but he's never been happy to be my steward. He's always wanted more." He paused. When no one else spoke, he continued. "Last summer, he approached me and asked to borrow a significant sum of money. He said he'd figured out how to harvest the crystals from the mountain, but he needed supplies from the city. I promised that if he managed it, I'd name him Esquire under me."

Peridot shifted closer to her mother, who dabbed at the corners of her eyes with a handkerchief.

"I swear to you, I had no idea what he had in mind. Over the past several months, he's gotten more and more distracted. He's made careless errors. I asked after his health, and he assured me he was well, just very busy preparing to harvest the crystals. Anyway, he sent me a message this morning telling me that both of you," Lord

Maksym gestured to Peridot and Kent, "were dead. He said the mine had collapsed, and he couldn't bear to return home and face his wife."

Kent leaned forward. "But wasn't that after he knew Bryoni and Simran had made it back here?"

"Yes. He was still trying to clear his name. I met him at a roadside inn to talk some sense into him and find out what had really happened. He confessed everything. He met the coastal sprites in Eriford when I sent him to check on my properties. He promised them a percentage of the crystals' selling price and told them they were free to hunt whatever trophy animals they wanted while they were here. He said he had no idea how you ended up with them, though." He looked to Simran.

"That's not much of a mystery, I'm afraid." Simran flushed and dropped his eyes to his smart leather shoes. "The coach I took from the city was robbed by bandits. Of course, you knew that already. They stole all our valuables and took us hostage." He drew a deep breath. "I helped lead an escape, and nearly everyone got away. One of them shot me in the leg, which is how they caught me again. They beat me senseless and dragged me with them from place to place until Peridot found me and freed me."

Lord Maksym chuckled, then grew serious. "That's basically the same story I heard from several others in town. It seems I owe you all an apology. If I hadn't loaned him that money, if I hadn't made that absurd promise of a title, none of this would have happened."

"Don't beat yourself up over it," Peridot's mother said gently. "If you hadn't loaned him the money, he would have gotten it somewhere else. I saw the same changes you did. He's been irritable and forgetful since the autumn. I even took him to Evanora twice to have her heal him, but it didn't work. Now I understand why."

The fire crackled on the hearth as the silence grew.

"Well, what now?" Kent asked. "What happens with Peridot's crystal?"

"What crystal?" Lord Maksym's face turned red, and he scowled fiercely.

"The dragons gave Peri—I mean Peridot, a crystal as a thank you for healing them."

Lord Maksym shifted in his seat, a look of wonder on his face. "May I…" he cleared his throat. "May I see it?"

Peridot rose and retrieved the crystal from her room. She set it in the center of the table, where it lit the space with a soft white glow.

All the sprites gathered around it, and even Peridot couldn't quite believe she'd received such a precious gift.

"I think it's up to Peridot what happens with this," Lord Maksym said after a thorough examination. "She may very well wish to keep it, since it was a gift from a dragon." He frowned at the crystal again. "…Exceedingly rare for them to give anything but burns to a sprite."

He wandered back to the sitting area and dropped back into her father's chair. "If you want to keep it, then it is yours. If you wish to sell it, I can help you procure a buyer. The reason your father wants these is that the prairie sprites have developed a sort of religion that centers on those crystals. They're willing to pay as much as five thousand gold pieces for an uncut crystal that size."

It was Peridot's turn to scowl. Wonder and excitement and dread mingled in her stomach. "Do I have to decide right now? That's more than my father made in his entire life, but I don't know that I'll ever get another gift from a dragon."

Her mother put an arm around her shoulders and guided her back to the worn sofa. "Of course, you can take your time, dear. I don't want you to do anything you'll end up regretting. Once it's gone, you can't get it back."

"I'll let you know as soon as I decide, Lord Maksym." Peridot let her mother ease her onto the sofa. "Will you expect a percentage of the sale price as a commission for finding a seller?"

"No. I think the trouble your family has been through more than pays any fees I might have considered."

"I have a different sort of question to ask." Simran grinned.

The mischievous look he shot her sent a jolt through Peridot.

"While we were trapped up on that mountain, I asked Peridot if she'd allow me to court her when we made it back here."

Angene gasped and glared at Peridot with murder in her eyes. Peridot sat frozen in shock.

Simran continued as if he hadn't noticed the sisters' reaction. "I made some, ah, questionable decisions up there, but I hope you don't think I'm such a dunderhead that you wouldn't still allow me to get to know you better?"

The anxiety in his voice made Peridot smile. "Yes, I'd like to get to know you better." She paused and made a show of thinking it over. "I think I'd like that quite a lot. Besides, you made some good decisions, too. Without your help, I wouldn't have found the baby or the eggs to return them to their mother."

A soft sniff came from the corner of the sofa where Peridot's mother sat.

"Are you all right, Mother?" Peridot asked. She hoped she hadn't completely ruined all her mother's plans. "This has been a hard day for you."

"Oh, yes, my dear. I'd all but given up hope that any young men would see how beautiful you are. I guess I just had to get out of your way." She sniffled and wiped her nose on her sleeve.

"I didn't help things along any, either." Peridot flushed. "Did I tell you I've decided to start going to lessons every day?"

Her mother squeezed her shoulders. "You did. You said so this morning, but you were probably too tired to remember much of that."

"I think it's the best thing you could possibly do." Kent reclined in his chair. "You've already proved you have a knack for healing. A bit of training and you'll be far better than Evanora."

Angene erupted in loud, mocking laughter, but choked off when no one joined in. "What, you mean little Peri might actually be good for something?"

"That's quite enough," their mother scolded. "Peridot has proved herself in these last few days. We were wrong to doubt her so much."

"I don't know that I'd go that far." Scalding heat filled Peridot's face. She fought the urge to hide behind her hands.

"I would. Based on what the others have said about how you handled yourself up there," her mother shot back. "And along those same lines, I've reconsidered your restriction. You're free to go to Bryoni's party, but I believe Hyacin said they're rescheduling it to next week, so Bry can recover a bit first."

A girlish squeal escaped Peridot before she clamped a hand over her mouth. "Wait 'til I tell Bryoni!" Her hand muffled the words, and everyone in the room laughed. Peridot met Simran's eyes and blushed even brighter at the gentle smile she saw there.

WOLVES

*L*ate the next morning, Peridot dressed in sturdy leather and grabbed Kent's old bow on the way out the door, since all of hers had been broken.

Her mother's voice stopped Peridot in her tracks. "Where are you off to? Surely you're not heading back up that mountain already?"

"I, well, I—"

"Yes?" Angene laughed, and Peridot flushed.

"I have to check on them. The wolves saved us a few times, and I want to make sure they're all right, and I want to see how the dragons react to me now."

Her mother scowled. "I don't think you should press your luck. Just because they let you heal the baby doesn't mean they'll let you close again." Her expression softened, and her voice dropped to a whisper. "I thought I lost you once. Don't you dare put me through that again."

Peridot couldn't stop the tears that burned hot streaks down her face. "I promise I won't put myself in danger. I hadn't really planned to go very high. I guess I was hoping they'd see me and come to say hello." She crossed the room and wrapped her arms around her mother's small frame. She hadn't done that in years, but she couldn't deny the comfort of her mama's embrace. They clung to each other for a long moment, and Peridot realized she didn't want to let go.

"Would you two knock that off? The world hasn't ended. We're all fine. Well, most of us, anyway." Angene sniffled. "Do you think we'll ever see him again?"

Peridot's mother dropped her arms and swiped at her face. Her voice came out stronger than Peridot expected. "I doubt he'll have the guts to show his face around here again, and I don't blame him for that. Now that the word's out that he invited slavers into our woods, every parent in town would be in line to have a swing at him."

"That's what I thought." Angene sniffled again and dabbed her nose on her sleeve.

"All right, I need to go so I can get back before supper. I'm hoping Simran might come by to eat with us." She stalked to the door and pulled it open, poised to sweep out into the morning sun, but she stopped short.

Simran stood in the doorway, his hand raised to knock. He laughed and stepped aside. "You're clearly on your way out, so instead of coming in, can I go with you?"

Peridot tried to fight the smile for half a heartbeat but gave in and grinned like a wolf with a venison haunch. "Don't you want to know where I'm going first?"

"I don't know that it really matters, but I'll bite. Where are you off to this morning?"

"To check on the wolves."

Simran blanched but quickly schooled his face into a mask of indifference. "So soon? You just made it home yesterday."

"I have to check on them. I didn't see any of them after the slavers brought out their poison, but I have to make sure."

"All right, then I'll go with you. You definitely shouldn't go alone." He nodded once. "And I promise to listen and do what you say."

Peridot grinned. "It's a deal." She turned her smile on her mother. "We'll be back in time to clean up for supper, I promise."

Peridot closed the door behind them and stepped out into the morning. She checked the dirt road for signs of eavesdroppers. No one was within earshot, but she dropped her voice to be sure. "You don't have to go. I won't hold it against you if you'd rather stay in town."

"I'm not letting you go alone. Not so soon." When Peridot opened her mouth to object, he rushed on. "I know you go up there by yourself all the time, but I didn't keep count of all the poachers. Are we completely sure there's none left up there?"

That brought Peridot up short. She'd tried to keep track, but she couldn't be sure she hadn't missed one or two. "All right. But if we see one, we head straight back to town. I'm not trying to take them on alone again."

"Deal."

They struck out down the gravel road. The rain had knocked down all the dust, but the warm sunshine had already dried out the worst of the mud. They strolled side by side in silence until they reached the edge of the forest.

"I want to apologize for the way I acted up here. I really don't have any excuse besides that I was stupid. Can you forgive me?"

"If I hadn't already forgiven you, I wouldn't have let you come with me." Peridot laughed. "And yes, I could stop you if I wanted to."

Simran chuckled but didn't push the issue. Instead, he offered his hand and helped her onto a small boulder. He hopped up after her and stood basking in the warm spring sunshine. "My uncle's not a bad guy, you know? I mean, I understand why you don't want to court him. I mean he's older than your—" He cut off abruptly. When he spoke again, his voice was low and rough, as if he were holding back some strong emotion. "I'm sorry. I didn't think that through."

Peridot drew a shaky breath. "My father. You can say it." She shook her head and swallowed against the knot in her throat. A fresh print in the dirt to her right grabbed her attention. "This way." She hopped down and took off at a brisk walk up the path.

The tracks led up the mountain to the same stream where she'd faced the bear. Peridot frowned. Had that really only been four days ago? She shook her head and stared at the spot where the wolf prints disappeared into the gently flowing water.

"My own father," she whispered. "How could he order the deaths of his children? I don't understand."

The emotions she'd held at bay since she'd discovered his involvement broke free, and the tears flowed like a river overrunning a dam. Her shoulders shook, but she blinked back the tears and picked up a heavy stone. She threw it hard at the nearest tree, letting some of her anger flow away with the effort. It didn't help. She repeated the process until the tears blinded her and strong arms held her from behind.

"It's all right. Here, sit down before you trip." He guided her gently to a fallen log and eased her onto it without taking his arms from around her.

Peridot struggled to contain her sobs, but the harder she tried to stop them, the harder she wept. "My own father wanted me dead," she whispered between ragged breaths.

"I don't know. Maybe he just got in too deep and didn't know how to dig back out." Simran's voice rose at the end as if he'd asked a question.

A hiccup escaped Peridot, and she clamped her lips closed until she was sure no more would follow. "I don't know. He sounded so certain."

"I never really met him, so I can't say for sure, but it's hard to believe he really meant what he said. I'm sure he's glad you're alive, even though it means he's essentially banished."

"You think so?" Peridot sniffled, bent over, and used the hem of her shirt to wipe her nose.

Simran dropped his hand from her shoulder to her waist. "I do. No father wants to see his children dead or sold off as slaves. And he never actually did anything to harm you, even when you were close enough for him to reach."

Peridot checked the position of the sun and sighed. "The day's getting away from us." She hiccupped again. "Let's go." She pushed herself to her feet and scanned the far bank for the trail. Her stomach sank when it didn't appear, but she pushed the panic aside. The wolves often waded up the stream and caught fish on the way back to their den. Sure enough, she picked up the trail a dozen paces to her right.

Around the trail's next bend, Peridot stopped. "There." Something big and gray moved between the trees ahead. She stared and tried to make out which wolf it was, but she couldn't tell from that distance.

Careful not to startle the animal—especially given the events of the past days—Peridot moved noisily toward the wolf, but stopped when she spotted another, and then another.

She held out a hand to stop Simran and crept forward alone. A tree provided a perfect vantage point, and she leaned slowly to the side until she could see the animals in the small clearing. They gathered around a patch of bare dirt, sniffing and whining. Peridot's breath left her in a pained cry. This was where she and Bryoni had buried the dead wolves.

Fresh tears stung her eyes and blurred her vision, but she stepped away from the tree and called out, her voice as soothing as she could make it. "Hey, loves. I know you miss them. I do too. Are the rest of you all right?"

The wolves stiffened and swung their heads toward her, then relaxed and whined again. In a rush of activity, the four canines rushed to her and nuzzled her face and arms.

"Can I join you? Will they allow it?"

"I think so. Just move slow and don't startle them. They're grieving." Her voice quivered on the last word, and Peridot cleared her throat.

Simran stepped up beside her and cocked his head to one side. "Grieving?"

"Yes. This is where we found the wolves the poachers killed." Peridot pointed to the bare patches. "Bry buried them here."

"Oh." Simran reached out a hand and scratched one of the enormous animals behind the ear. He gave a startled laugh when the wolf licked him with a tongue that covered half his face in one swipe.

Peridot relaxed and laughed along. "They've accepted you. They're pretty picky, so I'll take that as a sign."

"Oh? A sign of what?" Simran's eyes held an intensity that shot breathless excitement and warmth through Peridot's chest and down to her toes.

"That you're worth taking a chance on, maybe?"

He leaned in and cupped a hand behind her head. Moving so slowly she thought she'd go mad from anticipation, he inched closer until he pressed his lips against hers in a warm, gentle kiss. Peridot relaxed against him with a sigh and wrapped her arms around his waist.

Simran tilted his head and moved to deepen the kiss, but a long, furry nose pressed between them and shoved them apart. Peridot and Simran dissolved in laughter and both pet and scratched the wolf's ears.

"We should probably get back," Peridot said at last. "It's almost time to get ready for supper, and I don't want Mama to worry."

"Lead the way."

On the way back, Peridot answered a dozen questions about the wolves, how she told them apart, how she'd tamed them, and which were her favorites. Of course, she denied having any.

Dragons circled overhead when they stepped out of the forest and into the tall grass that separated the mountain from the village, but none swooped down or made any move toward Peridot. She shoved aside the faint disappointment that welled up in her belly.

It'll take time. It took three years with the wolves. At least we've made a start. She paused to watch them wheel and dive in the sky, and only proceeded toward home when they vanished around the mountain.

THE WEEK PASSED in a blur of lessons and practice and party preparations. Simran moved in with his uncle and visited Peridot at least every other day.

Peridot tipped her face up to the warm spring sun and smiled at the mountain's shadow across the valley. The pull of the wolves and dragons hadn't released its hold on her, but she hadn't yet returned to see how they'd recovered.

"Do you miss it? Oh, I'm sorry. I didn't mean to startle you." Peridot's mother set a hand on her shoulder. "Are you all right?"

Peridot flashed a sheepish smile. "I'm all right. I...Yes, I do miss it. I just want to learn a bit more before I go back."

"Well, it's almost time to get ready. Do you want me to do your hair?"

"That sounds perfect." Peridot linked arms with her mother and allowed herself to be led into the house.

PERIDOT'S first thought when she strolled into her friend's back garden was, *All of Bryoni's planning and stressing was worth it.* Lamps strung between trees and posts lit the area with a warm, inviting glow. The effect against the orange and red sunset took Peridot's breath away. The flowers Bryoni had spent the winter cultivating in her greenhouse scented the air with their fragrant perfume. Small tables filled with food dotted the areas around the open dance area. Peridot had spent the past three days helping Bryoni and her mother with the baking and cooking.

Peridot stood beside her mother and Kent as they waited their turn to speak with Bryoni and wish her the happiest of birthdays. She'd finished Bryoni's present while her mother did her hair, and she clutched the small package to her chest.

The line moved slowly, but Peridot spent the time tapping her foot to the music and admiring the scene. A small band had set up beside the dance floor. Only three couples twirled on the smooth wooden surface Bryoni's father had built, but the party hadn't fully gotten started yet. There would be plenty of time for dancing.

When they reached the front of the line, Peridot leaned in for a hug. "You look gorgeous!" And she did. Bryoni's brown eyes sparkled with happiness. Her soft pink hair shimmered in soft waves down her back, a stunning contrast to the deep green gown. Tiny beads sewn into the linen sparkled in the lamplight.

"So do you!" Bryoni squealed. "I'm so glad you got to come."

"Oh, so am I. Here, I brought this for you." Peridot handed her best friend the gift she'd spent so many hours making. "I'm dying to see how you like it."

"I know I'll love it. Thank you." Bryoni set the gift at the front of the table beside her. The simple brown linen looked shabby next to some of the others, but Peridot smiled at the place of importance Bryoni gave it.

Peridot hugged her friend again and stepped aside so the line could progress. Kent immediately went in search of Saika, the young woman he'd been courting since their adventure on the mountain.

"Ooh, I see Dahlia. Do you mind if I leave you on your own?" Peridot's mother smiled. "I want to ask how her new floors are working out, and that stuff bores you to tears."

"I'm fine. Go ahead." She watched her mother and Angene approach Dahlia, a woman a few years older than Peridot's mother but who remained as vibrant and energetic as any of the younger women.

"Peridot!"

Peridot glanced around to see who had called her. Lord Maksym and Simran strode toward her, cutting through the growing crowd with ease. Peridot stopped beside a table laden with sweet berry tarts and waited for the men. Lord Maksym leered at the low neckline of her gown, and Peridot cringed. She'd always managed to avoid him at parties before. She fought the urge to pull up her dress, though it was far from indecent. The square neckline showed the barest hint of cleavage below the silvery, moon-shaped pendant she always wore for special occasions. It was nearly as large as her palm, so it got in her way if she tried to wear it on a normal day.

"You're breathtaking." Simran grabbed her hand and bowed low over it.

Peridot smiled but fought the urge to roll her eyes at the exaggerated greeting. "Thank you."

"I've found a buyer for your crystal." Lord Maksym's announcement caught Peridot by surprise, and she frowned.

"Already? That seems really fast."

"They're very in demand in certain circles. He's willing to pay almost double what I told you before."

That proclamation did take Peridot's breath away, and several minutes passed before she could answer. "Double? I wouldn't know how to handle that much coin. Where would I keep it?"

"I'll help you figure out all the details. Don't worry about it just yet. Can I let him know you accept his offer?"

Peridot grinned. "Yes, definitely. Thank you so much for your help."

"It's the least I could do, really. I'll go send that message now." He scanned the crowd. "I'll return in an hour or so to enjoy the party." He ambled away, leaving Peridot and Simran alone in the middle of the crowd.

"Do you want to dance?" The uncertainty on Simran's face made Peridot smile. The differences between nephew and uncle were too numerous to count, and Peridot considered that a good thing.

"Yes, let's." She set her hand in his and strolled beside him onto the smooth wooden dance floor.

A song had just finished, so they waited for the band to begin the next set. The first notes sounded. A waltz. Her favorite dance.

Peridot smiled and moved to stand close to Simran. He set one hand on her waist and held her other hand in his. Together, they stepped into the dance.

They spun beneath the strings of lamps in the deepening night. Sights and sounds and smells blurred together in the beauty of the dance. Peridot couldn't imagine a better end to the adventures they'd shared in the forest. She focused on his face and realized she liked him more and more with every day. If nothing terrible happened, she might just have to marry him.